The
Diary of
Mademoiselle D'Arvers

TORU DUTT

Translated from the French by

N. KAMALA

Introduction by

G.J.V. PRASAD

PENGUIN BOOKS

PENGUIN BOOKS

Published by the Penguin Group

Penguin Books India Pvt. Ltd, 11 Community Centre, Panchsheel Park, New Delhi 110 017, India

Penguin Group (USA) Inc., 375 Hudson Street, New York, New York 10014, USA

Penguin Group (Canada), 90 Eglinton Avenue East, Suite 700, Toronto, Ontario, M4P 2Y3, Canada (a division of Pearson Penguin Canada Inc.)

Penguin Books Ltd, 80 Strand, London WC2R 0RL, England

Penguin Ireland, 25 St Stephen's Green, Dublin 2, Ireland (a division of Penguin Books Ltd)

Penguin Group (Australia), 250 Camberwell Road, Camberwell, Victoria 3124, Australia (a division of Pearson Australia Group Pty Ltd)

Penguin Group (NZ), cnr Airborne and Rosedale Roads, Albany, Auckland 1310, New Zealand (a division of Pearson New Zealand Ltd)

Penguin Group (South Africa) (Pty) Ltd, 24 Sturdee Avenue, Rosebank, Johannesburg 2196, South Africa

Penguin Books Ltd, Registered Offices: 80 Strand, London WC2R 0RL, England

First published as *Le Journal de Mademoiselle D'Arvers* by Didier, Paris 1879
This translation first published by Penguin Books India 2005

Translation copyright © N. Kamala 2005
Introduction copyright © G.J.V. Prasad 2005

Typeset in Perpetua by Mantra Virtual Services, New Delhi
Printed at Pauls Press, New Delhi

To my family

TRANSLATOR'S NOTE

Toru Dutt, a name synonymous with the first high quality Indian English writings in our country, was also fluent in French and wrote her first and perhaps only complete novel in that language, making her the first Indian also to have written in an European language other than that of our major (erstwhile) colonizer. Hence, it is not surprising for another Indian woman teaching French at present to be fascinated by her compatriot's writing in French as far back as the 1860s and 1870s! That her novel was practically unknown and unread was a source of regret but also a challenge to me. It seemed a crying shame that Toru Dutt's major prose contribution was not accessible to a larger audience, as a first translation done apparently in serialized form in a magazine long gone out of print, was not easily available. Neither was the original easy to procure as it was no longer in print and the only easily traceable and accessible copy was to be found in the Bibliothèque Nationale in Paris.

The agony and ecstasy of any translation is well known but it would be amiss of me if I did not state clearly what my approach was while translating this text. Translations are done but never well done, or so goes an old adage in French. However it is clear that one has an idea of what should be highlighted in a literary work. Are we to bring the book closer to the reader or bring the reader to the book? Should the translation read like one or should it read so fluently that there is no feel of the original? So many questions that decide what should be the final strategy adopted. Treading the fine line between a domesticating approach and a foreignising one, this translation has tried to make the text accessible, while trying not to let you forget that you are reading a *French* text.

To this end, the first translatorial decision was about names of characters. Marguerite, Guillaume, Véronique, to list but some of the names of characters in this novel, all have their English equivalents—Margaret, William, Veronica. In fact mention has been made in academic articles to this book as Margaret's diary. Changing the names would change the entire setting and tone of the book which is deliberately written in French, with French characters set in France. Converting the protagonist's name to Margaret, I felt, would give the erroneous impression of an English girl's story that takes place in France. Since this is not the case, the original names have been retained in all cases. Next comes the question of honorific titles like mademoiselle, madame, monsieur, and so on that are now comprehensible to most English speaking audiences and add to the colour and function as a special device to remind the reader that this is not an English story. So this translator's desire and attempt to maintain the original effect and not to anglicize it starts from the title of the book itself.

The next major question to be answered was who I was translating for, since this would dictate some of my linguistic choices. This version of the book is to be published in India, and since this is an Indian author writing in French, with an Indian translator, the language choice is English as used in India now. But this does not mean that it is completely contemporary in its usage. Toru Dutt's only short novel in English, *Bianca or the Young Spanish Maiden*, was used as a reference for certain spellings like Mamma, which would be close to the author's own style, without trying to attempt in vain that this should read like her book as *she would have written it if she had chosen to do so in English*. That would have been an almost unrealizable aim. My attempt is to give a glimpse of the original without making it so foreign that it would be an opaque text. On the one hand there was the matter of remaining close to the original French, on the other I had to struggle against my impulse to change certain sentences or phrases that crept up repeatedly in the text. The profusion of seemingly paragraph-long sentences, actually many long sentences separated only by semi-colons in a paragraph in the original which are natural to the genius of that language, have been shortened to smaller sentences so that the English readers do not get an unwarranted feel of excess that is not the effect in the French.

References to other texts have also been translated by me except for the passage from the Bible—Psalm CXIV in the original French but numbered Psalm CXVI in the English. The difference is in the Bible that must have been consulted. For the numbering is different even in French, depending on whether it is the Hebrew Bible or the Greek or the Vulgate. I have quoted from the King James' version. I chose to use this version instead of a more modern one in order to give a sense of an earlier time frame with its use of *thee* and *thou* which no longer figure in contemporary translations of the Bible. It seemed to reflect what would have been common usage in the nineteenth century.

These are but a few of the challenges that were before me when I undertook this wholly delightful and fulfilling task of translating the first ever known work of fiction in French written by an Indian in the nineteenth century.

N. Kamala

INTRODUCTION

Toru Dutt (1856–1877) is considered by many to be the first genuine Indian English poet. If she had not died at the young age of twenty-one, it is said with certainty that this is a poet whose works would have stood alongside the best poets in India and the world. As it is, her poem 'Our Casuarina Tree', is one of the most famous poems in Indian English and often singled out as the first major Indian English poem. But not many know that the talented Toru Dutt had many other writerly sides to her—apart from being a poet of the first order, she was an accomplished translator, essayist and novelist. Even fewer people know that she may be the first Indian woman to have written a novel in English (called *Bianca or the Spanish Maiden*[1]), and the novel whose translation you hold in your hands, which is perhaps the first novel written by an Indian in French![2]

Daughter of Govin Chunder Dutt (1828–1884) and Kshetramoni Dutt, Toru belonged to the illustrious Dutt family of Bengal. Her family tree reads like a genealogical account of pioneering Indian English writers. It is to Nilmony Dutt that the distinction of having bred such an accomplished family must belong. He was a well known and respected figure in Calcutta in the late eighteenth century. His eldest son, Rasomoy Dutt, was the secretary of the management committees of both the Hindu College and the Sanskrit College, and a judge of the

---

1. Originally serialized in 1878, *Bianca or the Young Spanish Maiden* is now available in book form edited by Subhendu Mund (Bhubaneswar: Prachi Prakashan, 2001).
2. There are any number of writers of the Indian diaspora who have written in French in recent years, but not only was Toru Dutt the first to write in French, her situation is also unique in that she is not a product of French colonization, but of the English.

Small Cause Court in Calcutta. To him were born Toru's father Govin, Hur and Greece Chunder Dutt, and Kylash, who is perhaps the author of the first recorded work of Indian English fiction. The poet-brothers, along with their nephew Omesh contributed to the famous *Dutt Family Album* (1870) which contains their original poems in English as well as many translations from French and German. Nilmony Dutt's youngest son, Pitambur, was the father of Ishan Chunder and Shoshee Chunder Dutt, both of whom wrote poetry in English. Shoshee Chunder Dutt is the more famous of the two, and wrote prolifically (poetry, essays and prose fiction). He is one of the more understudied and undervalued of Indian English writers of the nineteenth century. But it is the next generation of the Dutt family that is more (justly) famous. This consists of Toru Dutt and her equally illustrious cousin Ramesh Chunder Dutt (son of Ishan Chunder) who was the first Indian officer of the ICS. An eminent historian, a statesman and a nationalist who presided over the Lucknow Session (1899) of the Indian National Congress, he was a translator too, his translation of the Sanskrit epics enjoying fame till today.

Toru Dutt's family was Hindu when she was born, but embraced Christianity when she was six years old. While it is speculated that Kshetromoni, Toru's mother, may have been an unwilling participant in this conversion, she has translated *The Blood of Jesus* into Bangla. Toru's elder sister, Aru, was also an accomplished poet and translator, and contributed, along with Toru, to the collection of translations from French, *A Sheaf Gleaned in French Fields* (1876), which so impressed the famous English critic Edmund Gosse that he wrote: 'When poetry is as good as this, it does not matter whether Rouveyre prints it upon Whatman paper, or whether it steals to light in blurred type from some press in Bhowanipore.'[3]

Thus it was that Toru grew up in a literary environment. Her father ensured that his daughters were educated at home and were trained in music and dance. Toru could play the piano and was an accomplished

---

3. Edmund Gosse, Introduction to *Ancient Ballads and Legends of Hindustan*, x.

horsewoman. In 1865 Toru's brother, Abju, died of consumption at the tender age of fourteen. Govin Chunder Dutt decided that his family needed to put this tragedy behind them, and sailed for Europe in 1869. The family stayed in France for a period of four months only in Nice, where Toru and Aru were tutored in French. The remarkable translations from French were sparked off by this brief stay, a stay which was long enough for Toru to declare herself as a steadfast French woman. Though hardly thirteen years old at that time, she took a great interest in French literature as well as politics, as evidenced by Clarisse Bader in her Introduction to the original French publication of this novel.

In 1870 the family arrived in England, where they spent some time in London before shifting to Cambridge in 1871. The girls continued with their education throughout, even attending lectures for women at Cambridge. Aru's illness drove the family back to India in 1873, because Govin Chunder didn't think that either girl would be able to withstand another winter in Europe. It was at Cambridge that Toru met her lifelong friend Mary Martin; it is in her letters to Mary that we actually come to receive a personal portrait of Toru. [4] It is to Mary that Toru wrote on the death of her sister Aru in 1874 that, 'The Lord has taken Aru from us. It is a sore trial for us, but His Will be done. He doeth all things for our good.' In these letters, Toru comes across as a deeply religious and moral person, warm, lively and caring.

The death of Aru and Toru's illness put paid to Govin Chunder Dutt's plan to emigrate to Europe. Toru devoted herself to her writing fully, completing the translation project that she and Aru had begun in London years earlier. She published essays on Le Conte de Lisle and Henry Derozio in the *Bengal Magazine* in 1874. Both the poets seem apt choices for a pioneering Indian English writer to critique—for

---

4. Some of Toru Dutt's letters have been included in Eunice de Souza and Lindsay Pereira (eds.), *Women's Voices: Selections from Nineteenth and Early-Twentieth Century Indian Writing in English* (New Delhi: OUP, 2002). For all her letters and other details, see Harihar Das, *Life and Letters of Toru Dutt* (London: OUP, 1921).

both are her predecessors in writing in European languages even while they were 'Asiatic of half-caste poets' as she says in her article on the former. Toru Dutt also published 'A Scene from Contemporary History' in the *Bengal Magazine* in 1975—this was a translation of speeches and poems by Victor Hugo and M. Thiers. She also began to learn Sanskrit in December 1875. *A Sheaf Gleaned in French Fields* came out on 24 March 1876. In the meanwhile she was desirous of translating Clarisse Bader's *La Femme dans l'Inde Antique*, and wrote to her for permission, enclosing with it a copy of *A Sheaf*. This letter was received by Clarisse Bader on 2 February 1877, and thus began the brief correspondence between her and Toru Dutt.

Toru became increasingly unwell, and died of consumption on 30 August 1877. She was buried in the Christian Missionary Society Cemetery in Calcutta. Her wish to meet Clarisse Bader and to translate her work were both unfulfilled. It is not an exaggeration to state that this prodigy was capable of work of the highest literary quality, and that her unfortunate early death robbed the literary firmament of a dazzling star.

Toru's father Govin Chunder Dutt discovered the manuscripts of her two novels after her death. While he published her English novel, *Bianca*, in serial form in the *Bengal Magazine* in 1878 (January to April), he sent the French novel, *Le Journal de Mademoiselle D'Arvers*, to Clarisse Bader in August 1878 to arrange for its publication. The novel was published in 1879 by Didier, Paris, with an introduction by Clarisse Bader. The novel received some good reviews, but is now an almost forgotten curiosity born of the colonial encounter. In 1882, *Ancient Ballads and Legends of Hindustan*, Toru Dutt's famous collection of poems, was published from London with an introduction by Sir Edmund Gosse. This firmly established her reputation as a poet. E. J. Thompson wrote of her that, 'Toru Dutt remains one of the most astonishing women that ever lived, a woman whose place is with Sappho and Emily Bronte, fiery and unconquerable of soul as they.' He said that her poems show her breaking free of the fetters of convention and feeling her way to freer rhythms, and that her poems 'are sufficient to place Toru Dutt in the small class of women who have written English verse that can stand.'[5]

But what is the verdict on Toru Dutt the novelist? Recent criticism on Toru Dutt's poetry as well as her prose (her letters) demonstrates the making of an 'individual, and essentially modern, voice.'[6] This is not seen as true of her English novel, *Bianca*. As a matter of fact, controversy surrounds the manuscript of *Bianca*, which was published as an unfinished novel by Govin Chunder. It has been suggested that Govin Chunder 'actively prevented the dissemination of the manuscript of *Bianca*' by publishing it in serial form in the *Bengal Magazine* instead of having it published in England, which would have ensured a larger circulation and higher visibility.[7] Govin Chunder does say in a brief note appended to the last part of the serial that in his view *Bianca* was unfinished and abandoned by Toru because 'the novel left in the French language is very much superior indeed to this fragment and is complete.'[8] Thus his defence would be that he did his best for what was essentially a fragment of a novel. The 'superior' and 'complete' French novel was published by Didier, a leading publishing house in Paris.

But all this begs a few important questions. Why did Toru write these novels in secret? Her father had been very supportive of her other enterprises; why did she hide her novels from him? Was even the French novel complete in the sense that it was revised and ready for publication, or was it still an early version? Did Toru want to publish the novels at all? If they were not meant to be published, why did Toru

5. Quoted in Harihar Das, p. 220.

6. Rosinka Chaudhuri, *Gentlemen Poets in Colonial Bengal: Emergent Nationalism and the Orientalist Project* (Calcutta: Seagull Books, 2002), p.167. See this book and G.J.V. Prasad, *Continuities in Indian English Poetry: Nation, Language, Form* (New Delhi: Pencraft International, 1999) for a critical placement of the poetry of the Dutts and other poets of the era.

7. Malashri Lal, *The Law of the Threshold: Women Writers of Indian English* (Simla: Indian Institute of Advanced Study, 1995), p. 38.

8. Quoted in Subhendu Mund (ed.), *Toru Dutt's Bianca*, p. 16.

write them? In a sense, all writing is of therapeutic value to writers; were these novels therapeutic for Toru Dutt? How exactly? Is the answer to this question to be found in the last question I want to raise here, which is, why are both the novels set outside India in the West, and peopled completely by European characters?

In a letter to her friend Mary Martin, written ironically on the same day that saw the publication of *A Sheaf Gathered in French Fields*, Toru complains:

> We do not go much into society now. The Bengali reunions are always for men. Wives and daughters and all women-kind are confined to the house, under lock and key, à la lettre, and Europeans are generally supercilious and look down on Bengalis. I have not been to one dinner party or any party at all since we left Europe. And then I do not know any people here except those of our kith and kin, and some of them I do not know.

In a later letter dated 31 October 1876 Toru says that she does not visit anyone at all and that her ways would be considered, 'infra dig, unladylike, immodest' by others. She writes that it is only in Baugmaree that she can be herself, 'without fear of any peering and scandalised neighbour, staring in surprise and contempt at my "strange manlike ways".' These two letters point to why Toru Dutt wrote her novels in secret, and why she set them in Europe and peopled them with European characters. Both the novels are romances; they trace the destinies of young women in love. For this to happen, for women to have choice in their lives, they need not just personal space but freedom in social intercourse. Neither would really have been available in the Bengali society of Toru Dutt's times.

If even Toru Dutt, a Christian and daughter of the liberal Govin Chunder Dutt, a member of the famous Dutt family, could not attend parties or interact with men in social gatherings, how could she imagine other Indian girls (of her class or otherwise) meeting men and falling in love? While she may have been simply embarrassed by her body's awakening and the desires of her adolescence and youth to share her fiction with her father, she could definitely not see how love could be found or nurtured in her clime. As for many Indians of her generation and after, all possibilities that could only be achieved by forsaking Indian conventions and traditions were in the West. In her case certainly, a girl could have romance only in the West; it was there that she could have choice and be free to listen to and express her heart. And it was in the West, and through a western heroine, that Toru Dutt could explore the bodily passions of a young woman, her fears and her desires. Is this why Clarisse Bader notes that the heroine of the French novel resembles the author whom she had never seen? And is this why she could not show the novels to her father?

While it is not clear as to when Toru Dutt actually wrote her two novels, it seems to me that since *Bianca* begins with the death of the elder sister of the heroine, and since *Le Journal* has the long shadow of the heroine's death visible in its latter half, that both novels were written in Calcutta after their return from Europe, and perhaps after Aru's death, the English novel preceding the French; but this is mere speculation. In any case these novels were written by a young author who was eager for life and yet afraid of what it may bring. In *Bianca*, the author cannot imagine the fruition of the passionate love affair; the novel ends with the postponed promise of a marriage with the hero leaving for the Crimean War. In *Le Journal*, she finds that she can imagine many things including a happy marriage (even here she cannot see how the heroine can work out when her child would be born; it is the husband who gives her the information) but cannot imagine it to be long-lasting—death is always in the air. Clarisse Bader points out in her Introduction the ways in which the novel betrays its Indian origin; perhaps the characters who betray the personal nature of the exploration are the fathers of the two heroines. In both the novels, the fathers are kind and supportive of their daughters. However, in *Bianca*, the father is a stifling figure who has to fight his own tendencies to hold on to his motherless daughter. Having lost his other children, he wants to retain Bianca with himself forever. Was that another reason for not showing the English novel to her father?

Whatever be the reasons for her suppression of the two novels during her lifetime, there is no reason left now for their continued invisibility. While *Bianca* has been edited and reissued recently, *Le Journal* has waited for this edition to be available in book form in English. Nineteenth century Indian literature needs further archival work and critical scrutiny, and I hope that this translation will contribute to interest in the area and also to the recognition of the unique talents of Toru Dutt: a truly bilingual writer but with the characteristic ironic postcolonial twist, whose bilingual creative competence is in two colonial languages—English and French! She was heir to three traditions, distanced from, even while feeling herself at home in each, making her creative choices from all three in order to construct her own identity. In *Le Journal* you have a unique product of the colonial encounter: a novel in French during the days of British dominance of India (a complete escape into another, albeit colonial, territory), a truly moral Christian novel of love, marriage, death and reconciliation written by an Indian who was Hindu by birth, and a French novel that was dedicated by fond father to the English Viceroy of India, Lord Lytton.

New Delhi
G.J.V. Prasad

Le Journal de Mademoiselle D'Arvers

(The Diary of Mademoiselle D'Arvers)

INTRODUCTION TO THE
ORIGINAL FRENCH EDITION

Her Life and Her Works

On 2 February 1877, I received through the intermediary of my editors, a letter addressed to me from Calcutta. The letter came from a young Hindu girl who asked me permission to translate one of my works—*La Femme dans l'Inde Antique* (*Women in Ancient India*).

A book accompanied this letter—it was a collection of French poetry translated into beautiful English verse—*A Sheaf Gleaned in French Fields, (Une gerbe glanée dans les champs français)*.

The author of the letter and of the book that I received at the same time was already famous, despite her youth, in her country and even in England. She was called Toru Dutt. Member of a Christian family, she was the daughter of Babu Govin Chunder Dutt, a respectable magistrate and a learned scholar of Calcutta.

This message from India was the beginning of a correspondence that was established between Toru Dutt and myself, and was interrupted too soon by the death of this interesting young girl. This correspondence which was published in Calcutta by Babu Govin Chunder Dutt,[1] the letters that this loyal and bereaved father wrote to me after the death of his daughter, and finally the biographical note with which he preceded a new edition of *A Sheaf Gleaned in French Fields*—all this material allowed me to understand the traits of a truly remarkable physiognomy. I will try to reproduce them here.

---

1. *A Sheaf Gleaned in French Fields*, by Toru Dutt. A new edition, Bhowanipur, 1878. Prefatory Memoir, p. xix-xxvi.

Toru Dutt was born in Calcutta on 4 March 1856. In 1869, she came to Europe with her family and remained here for four years.

Toru and her elder sister Aru spent some months in a boarding house in France. In England, they assiduously followed the readings meant for women at the University of Cambridge.

When the Babu returned to Calcutta with his family, he taught Toru the ancient brahmanical idiom of Sanskrit. He always appears to us as the study companion of his daughter. In a charming domestic picture, he shows us how the hours of study were spent in the patriarchal house on Maniktollah Street:

'She read a lot,' he says talking of Toru. 'She read very fast too, but when she read she never skimmed over any difficulty. Dictionaries, lexicons and encyclopedias were consulted until the difficulty was resolved, and a note was later taken down. This resulted in explanation of difficult words and sentences being imprinted in her brain, so to say, and when we had a discussion about the meaning of a term or a sentence in Sanskrit, or French, or German, she was proved to be right eight times out of ten. Sometimes I was so sure of my fact that I used to say, "Well, let us take a bet." The bet was normally for a rupee. But when the authorities were consulted, she was almost always the winner. It was very curious and amusing for me to observe her when she lost. First it would be a brilliant smile; then her nimble fingers tapped my grizzled cheeks, and then she would perhaps quote from Mrs Barrett-Browning, her favourite poet, some passage like this— "Ah! My comrade, you are older and more learned, and you are a man";—or some such similar pleasantry.'[2]

With what satisfaction the father effaces himself before the scholar and admits being beaten by his daughter! What touching pride in the confession of these frequent defeats! The Babu initiating his daughter into European studies, and also into the ancient brahmanical language that even the ancient Indian women did not speak.[3] Isn't that a

---

2. Prefatory Memoir (in the cited work), p. xi.
3. Instead of Sanskrit, the Indian women spoke the language of the lower classes, Prakrit.

magnificent result to the influence exerted in modern India by Christian civilization, and which extends even to the sectors of Brahmanism and Islamism? According to Mr Garcin de Tassy, 'Hindu, Muslim, and Parsi Indians found themselves at their own cost, schools conducted in the European system, not only for boys but also for girls, a thing unheard of till now.'[4]

Toru Dutt did not direct her studies towards history. One day, lord L . . . visited the Babu and his family in Calcutta, and having surprised Aru with a novel in her hand, he told the two girls, 'Ah! You should not read too many novels, you should read histories.'

Toru replied, 'We like to read novels, lord L . . .'

'Why?'

The bright young girl replied smilingly, 'Because novels are true, and histories are false.'[5] Gaily proposing this paradox, Toru Dutt showed herself to be a true daughter of the poetic Hindu race that likes to replace history with legend.

Toru loved the old Sanskrit poets. In one of her charming letters written in French to me, I read the following words, 'I cannot say, mademoiselle, how much your affection (for you love them, your book and your letter are witness enough of that) for my compatriots and my country touch me; and I am proud to say that the heroines of our great epics are worthy of all honour and all love. Is there a heroine more touching and more lovable than Sita? I don't think so. When I hear my dear mother singing in the evening, the old songs of our

---

4. Course on Hindustani in the Ecole de langues orientales vivantes (School of Living Oriental Languages). Opening speech of 6 December 1869. Garcin de Tassy followed with great interest the education of women in India, and often renders a well deserved homage to Miss Carpenter who speeded them up so powerfully. The eminent professor initiates us on this progress in the journal dedicated each year to the language, literature and mores of the Hindus, and which is truly the history of civilization in modern India. A few days after these lines were written, Mr Garcy was no more of this world, and his beautiful soul so Christian went to join his beloved companion who had preceded him in blessed eternity.

5. Prefatory Memoir, p. x.

country, I almost always cry. The lament of Sita, when, banished for the second time, she wanders about in the forest, all alone, with despair and dread in her heart, is so pathetic that, I think there is nobody, who can hear it without crying.'

This same letter enclosed two translations from the Sanskrit into English whose brisk concision struck me. They were two episodes of the *Vishnu Purana: la Légende de Dhruva* (*The Legend of Dhruva*) and *le Royal Ascète et la Biche* (*The Royal Ascetic and the Doe*).

Reared on the vibrant ancient tales sung by her mother, initiated by her father to the study of Sanskrit, will Toru Dutt sing of her country? Will Hindustani be the instrument of her poetic genius? Will she describe the marvelous landscapes of India, the virgin forest where lush vegetation flourishes? Like the old Sanskrit poets, will she delight in following the gazelle in its light race, in surprising the glorious flight of the hummingbirds, those winged gems? Will she hear, in the thick jungles, under the arcade of the nyagrodha, the fig tree of India, the sweet song of the koel, the hissing of the serpent, the roar of the tiger? Will she contemplate the lakes inhabited by swans and covered with blue water lilies and *nelumbos* with rose petals? Will she say how, under the tropical sun's rays, the mountains with torrents of spray, make the metals gleam, and how, under the brilliant light of a sapphire sky, the eternal snows of the Himalayas sparkle with diamond lights?

No, in front of these pictures painted by Valmiki and Vyasa, our young Christian Hindu turns towards our pale Occident where nature is less imposing, but where man is bigger, and appropriating with a slight modification, what Schiller says of the *Jeune Fille étrangère* (*Young Foreign Girl*), she says in these verses that she gives as epigraph to *A Sheaf Gleaned in French Fields*:

'I *bring* flowers and fruits plucked in a different soil, under the light of a different sun, in a happier nature.'

Ich *bringe* Blumen mit und Fruchte,
Gereift auf einer andern Flur,
In einem andern Sonnenlichte,

In einer glucklichern Natur.[6]

Toru Dutt delighted in interpreting the songs of our French poets, but as we have already said, this young Indian girl, quite enamoured of our European civilizations, translated these songs, not into Hindustani, but into English, and that is why instead of increasing the number of women poets from India that is made known to us, thanks to the elegant pen of Mr Garcin de Tassy, Toru Dutt has taken her place among the writers of England.

It is not however the accents of our classical poets that our young Hindu girl would like to translate. Our seventeenth century writers, in whom reason takes precedence over sentiment, and for whom poetry is but a transparent crystal through which thought can be read, our seventeenth century authors did not captivate this young child born in a country where poetry, all sentiment and imagination, has the exuberance of a tropical nature. What attracts this young girl is the poetry of the nineteenth century. In it she finds what her compatriots have always liked—the bright and dramatic reproduction of the movements of the heart, an abundance of images, and the richness of colour. It is not surprising to see what literary admiration Victor Hugo inspires in her. In the interesting notes that accompany her translations, she cries out with enthusiasm: 'It would be absurd not to make a single comment on Victor Hugo in a short note at the end of a book. His name is among the great of this earth. Along with Shakespeare, Milton, Byron, Goethe, Schiller, and the others, his place has long been marked in the Valhalla of poets.'[7]

Even though Toru Dutt's rich imagination placed the poetic genius of Victor Hugo above that of Lamartine, her religious soul recognized, however, the moral superiority of the poet of *Méditations* and of

---

6. Schiller had said:
    Sie brachte Blumen und Fruchte, etc.
    (*Das Madchen aus der Fremde.*)

7. *A Sheaf Gleaned, etc.* note xxxii.

Harmonies. 'In fantasy, in imagination, in brilliance, in grandeur, in style, in all that makes a poet, except in purity, he must bow to Victor Hugo,' she says. 'In purity, he is second to none. His mind is essentially religious. He never forgot what he had learned in the lap of his dear mother, a mother he remembered with love a thousand times in his writings.'[8]

Later, in a note dedicated to de Laprade, Toru Dutt says thus: 'Laprade and Lamartine are the only great modern poets of France whose works are essentially and eminently pure and religious, and it is remarkable that both of them were deeply indebted to their mothers for the direction their minds took, women of prayer, large-minded and self-denying.'[9]

Along with Lamartine and Victor Hugo and de Laprade, we find in the translations and notes of Toru Dutt almost the whole of the contemporary Parnassus: Béranger, Pierre Lebrun, Alfred de Musset, Alfred de Vigny, madame de Girardin, Sainte-Beuve, Brizeux, Ponsard, Théophile Gautier, Autran, Reboul, M/s Auguste Barbier, Emile Augier, L. Ratisbonne, Leconte de Lisle, F. de Gramont, Eugène Manuel, François Coppée, André Lemoyne, Sully-Prudhomme, Joséphin Soulary, etc., etc.

But it wasn't sufficient for Toru Dutt to translate our poets—she wanted to be a *French* writer. Among the manuscripts left by her figures a novel that the young Hindu had written in French—it is *Le Journal de Mademoiselle D'Arvers (The Diary of Mademoiselle D'Arvers)*, which we are publishing today and we will talk about later.

Toru Dutt did not just strive to like our language, our literature. She loved our country, and she showed her love at precisely that moment when France was dying. In pages that did not see the light of day, this young child who had not yet turned fifteen, this Asiatic, retraced our patriotic sufferings with an anguished accent that anyone would say belonged to a French girl. She was then in London. Allow

---

8. *A Sheaf Gleaned, etc.* note li.

9. *Ibid.* note liv.

me to translate what she wrote on 29 and 30 January 1871, in the unpublished diary of her voyage:

'29 January 1871. London. No. 9, Sydney Place, Onslow Square. It has been a long time since I wrote in my diary. What changes have taken place in France since the last time I took this diary in my hand! Alas! What changes have taken place in France! When we were in Paris for a few days, how beautiful it was! What houses! What roads! What a magnificent army! But now! Ah! How it has fallen! It was the first of the cities, but now what misery it houses! As soon as the war began, my whole heart was with the French,[10] even if I was sure of their defeat. One evening, when the war was on and the French had had a lot of loss, I heard Papa say something to mama regarding the emperor. I bolted down, and I learnt that the French had capitulated. The Emperor and his whole army had surrendered to Sedan. I remember clearly how I went up the stairs and how I recounted it to Aru, half suffocating, half crying . . .

'Capitulated! That is a word the French use with difficulty! Poor, poor people, they must have been hard pressed to have surrendered! Then came other thunderbolts—a revolution in Paris, the Empress flying away to England, the imperial prince sent to Wilhelmshohe as prisoner of war, the Germans marching into Paris, Strasbourg bombarded and capitulating. What misery in this town during the bombarding! All the houses devastated! Bombs flying about everywhere! Then it was the turn of Metz . . .

'I am still an unshakeable French, or rather should I say, an unshakeable French woman. I will not be inconstant, even if the French are defeated. I am with them in all my sympathies and all my sentiments. Now Paris is bombarded, and she will have to surrender in a day or two. It is almost five months that she has been under siege. I am happy to learn of her capitulation, for then, I hope there will be no more bloodletting. How many thousands of people have realized the words

---

10. Around the time we read these words, H.R.H. the Prince of Wales said in almost the same words: 'My whole heart is with France.'

of the poet:

> To die for the country,
> Is the most beautiful destiny,
> The most worthy of envy.

'Alas! Thousands and thousands of men have shed blood from their hearts for their country, but however the country fell into the hands of their enemies. Is it because many were deeply plunged in sin and no longer believed in God? But however there were and there are thousands who fear God. Oh France, France, how you have fallen! May it happen that after this humiliation, you serve and adore God better than what you did these days! I hope that there will soon be peace and no more blood will be shed . . .

'30 January. Monday. The lunch bell rang when we were dressing. We went down, and Salvageot, an Italian domestic servant of our house, told us that Paris had capitulated . . . I read in *The Times* that it was so. "The Germans will enter the forts tomorrow," such read the telegramme. I suppose right now they would have entered. They will disarm all the regiments except for the sedentary national guards and one division that will take it upon themselves to quell all tumult or all battle in the streets while the Germans enter Paris . . . Poor, poor France, how my heart bleeds for you!'[11]

In the pages written by this young girl from India, I find with emotion the same poignant anguish, the same heartbreak, the same thoughts of national expiation and patriotic recovery that I myself went through during that period in an unpublished diary. Yes, it was very much a French girl's heart that beat, in unison with ours, in the breast of this young Asian, and one that *bled* in the grip of our sorrows.

In the pages that we have just translated, Toru Dutt names her elder sister Aru whose name we have already mentioned. The two sisters were united by tender affection and an accordance of tastes.

---

11. *Extracts from Toru's private diary,* manuscript.

Both of them knew how to combine the humble care of domestic life with serious study and poetic works. But despite being the eldest, Aru effaced herself in front of her sister, and always followed the latter's impulse. A photograph we have in front of our eyes reproduces well the different attitudes of the two sisters. The gentle Aru, calm and collected, is seated, whereas, standing next to her and seeming to cover her with affectionate protection, Toru, radiant with vivacity under her superb hair falling on her shoulders, shoots a fiery look from her black eyes.

Aru too wanted to pay her tribute to French literature. Among other poems she had translated the *Jeune Captive* ('Young Captive'). She had reproduced this ode with surprising fidelity, in English verse, which rivals in elegance and grace the French verse of Chénier. She too could have said like Aimée de Coigny:

> I am but in spring, I want to see the harvest;
> ....
> Brilliant on my branch and the honour of my garden,
> I have but seen only the lights of the morning,
> I want to finish my day.
> ....
> I do not want to die as yet.

Publishing *A Sheaf Gleaned in French Fields* in 1876, Toru Dutt said, 'The author of these pages has only to add that the pieces signed just A. are of her dear and only sister's, who went to sleep into Jesus on 23 July 1874, prematurely at the age of twenty . . . If she had lived, this book would have been better with her help, and the author would have less reason to feel ashamed, and less occasion to crave the indulgence of the reader. Alas! Among the saddest words in language and of the pen are the following—it could have been.'[12]

When Toru Dutt penned these lines she was already suffering the

---

12. *A Sheaf Gleaned, etc.,* note clxvi, and 2nd edit., note ccix.

effects of the same illness that took away her sister. Since the second of the letter she wrote to me in 1877, she talked to me of a persistent cough which never left her. One day, she made me look forward to her forthcoming arrival in Paris—her father wanted to consult for her sake the doctors of France and England.

But it was in vain that this poor father, who had already lost two children, wanted to snatch from death his last remaining daughter. Toru's illness progressed so rapidly that it was impossible to transport her to Europe. On 30 July, with the illusion left by the illness of the chest till the last moments, Toru wrote to me with a feeble hand: 'I was very ill, dear mademoiselle, but the good Lord had answered my parents' prayers and I am recovering slowly. I hope to write in length soon.'

She was to write no longer to me, and she could have repeated this gentle French verse that she had written to me in a letter with a touching and melancholic grace:

'Adieu then, my friend that I never knew.'[13]

Without ever having seen Toru, I loved her. Her letters revealed a candour, a sensitivity, a charm of goodness and of simplicity that had made her dear to me and that showed me the native qualities of the Hindu woman developed and transformed by the Christian civilization of Europe. And how could I have ever remained insensible to affection so spontaneous and so bright that was shown to me from beyond far away seas, by a descendant of the Indian women who had inspired the work of my twenty-second year?

I wrote to Toru to congratulate her on her recovery. I requested her to congratulate her mother and her father on my behalf. I inserted in my letter a flower taken from a bouquet placed in front of the statue of the Notre Dame des Victoires (Our Lady of Victory). It was a rodanthe, the pretty rose plant with a silver calyx that lives forever

---

13. Lefèvre-Deumier.

like the everlasting flower of which it is a variety. Alas! When I sent this souvenir to Toru Dutt, my friend from India had already been dead for a few days. Her parents were to read with what distress the felicitation that I had addressed to them about her recovery, and the everlasting rose flower that I had sent her as the pious and smiling emblem of a still living friendship, became like the other everlasting flower, the flower of a tomb!

'She left us on the evening of 30 August for the place where separation and chagrin are unknown,' wrote Toru Dutt's father to me. 'Her faith in her Saviour was without reservations, and her spirit was always in perfect peace, peace that is beyond all understanding. It is the physical pain of the vesicatory that drag the tears from my eyes.' She said once to the doctor, "but my spirit is at peace. I know to whom I am entrusting myself." There was never a gentler child, and she was my last. My wife and I, in our old age, are left in an empty, desolate house which earlier echoed the voices of our three beloved children, but we have not been abandoned—the Comforter is with us, and a time will come when we will meet again in the presence of our Lord to be never separated again.'

A few days before writing the letter to me, a page of which I have just translated, the generous Christian who wrote to me had thus ended the biography of his daughter Toru:

> Why were these three young lives so full of hope and work so suddenly cut off, whereas I, old and infirm, I live a languishing life? I think, I can obscurely see that there is a concordance here, a preparation, needed for the future life that they possess and that I do not as yet possess. One day I will see everything clearly. May the Lord be blessed. May His will be done.[14]

In the face of such an èlan of faith, how can one not recognise and salute the paternal influence to which we owe Toru Dutt?

---

14. Prefatory Memoir, p. XXVII. (*A Sheaf Gleaned, etc.*)

Soon after the death of the young Hindu, the *Calcutta Review* published eight sonnets that Toru Dutt had translated of one of her favourite French poets, le comte de Gramont. The last of these sonnets says how, thanks to divine grace, the force of the ill Christian is perfected even in weakness. We can sense how the translator must have appropriated for herself these verses to express her pious personal resignation. After having inserted the eight poems, the *Calcutta Review*, applying to the young dead woman the last words of the first sonnet, reminded us that it was the generous warmth of divine love that had flowered in the skies, the bud prematurely cut off on earth.

The *Review* that we have just quoted, stood out among the other reviews in England and in India that paid homage to the literary talent of Toru Dutt and considered her premature end as a great loss to literature. 'She wrote in English,' said the review, 'with all the delicacy and all the good taste of an English woman of high education, and many of her small poems use gentle eloquence, half melancholic, and a depth of religious sentiment, illuminated by a high and pure imagination, which promised to obtain for her an honoured place among the English poets of the present epoch.'[15]

In France, the illustrious Indologist whose kind name we have cited more than once, Garcin de Tassy, member of the Institute, president of the Asiatic Society of Paris, paid a public homage to this young memory: 'On 30 August,' he said, 'Toru Dutt died in Calcutta, a young Hindu, hardly twenty years old, the little prodigy who already knew at that age, not only Sanskrit, her sacred language, but English and French, that she wrote and spoke in a pure manner, which is not altogether surprising since she was brought up in Europe. But, what is more remarkable, at an age when young people are still at school, she had already published English poetry stamped with genius and of an astonishing purity of style. Lately, she had brought out a volume in-octavio entitled *A Sheaf Gleaned in French Fields*, it is a choice of French poetry translated by her in excellent English verse. This young *purebred*

---

15. Editor, *Calcutta Review*, 1877

Hindu, as she wrote to me herself, but converted to Christianity, was the last daughter who remained for Babu Govin Chunder Dutt, Honorary Magistrate and Justice of the Peace in Calcutta. He had lost another daughter twenty years old as well, equally gifted, and who also died of consumption like her.'[16]

Lord Lytton, Viceroy of India, was among the first to express his deep sympathy to Babu Govin Chunder Dutt on his loss. Worthy heir of a name as illustrious in letters as in diplomacy, himself a rare poet, Lord Lytton, author of *Clytemnsestre*, had one more title to his name to deplore the death of this young girl that England considered a poet of great promise—that of Lord Lytton, son of a distinguished *authoress*, who took delight in honouring the woman with gifts of intelligence.[17] It was to the Viceroy of India that Babu Govin Chunder Dutt dedicated his daughter's posthumous and unpublished book, *Le Journal de Mademoiselle D'Arvers (The Diary of Mademoiselle D'Arvers)*.[18]

It was not without emotion that I received a copy of Toru Dutt's manuscript, copy entirely due to her old father's hand: 'My hand trembles and I am forced to copy slowly,' wrote the Babu to me as he set himself to this long task. Nothing in this beautiful and firm handwriting betrays this trembling. We can see that the father found strength in the accomplishing of the task, cruel and kind at the same time, which gave him the dear illusion: 'All the time that I copy, I feel that I am conversing with her,' he wrote.

The Diary of Mademoiselle D'Arvers, whatever may have been the

---

16. These lines end the last annual review published by Garcin de Tassy. I said earlier, in note 4, that the dear and venerable master died at the very moment that I had finished the present note.

17. Lord Edward-Robert Lytton is the son of the famous author of *The Last Days of Pompeii* and of Lady Lytton-Bulwer, who published spiritual studies of social mores. The Viceroy of India is also the nephew of Lord Henry Lytton, the ambassador who wrote in particular such remarkable works on the social and political mores of France.

18. Other than the works we have cited, Toru Dutt left in manuscript form original English poetry and eight chapters of an English novel.

French inspiration and form, makes us think of those exotic flowers transplanted in our countries, and which, however acclimatised they may be, still retain the perfume of their native place. India's influence can be seen here. The passionate devotion felt by Marguerite d'Arvers for the fiancé turned criminal, recalls not just the charity of the Gospels, it is also the memory of those ancient Brahmanical mores which makes a woman prostrate before a happy or unhappy, innocent or guilty husband. We also recognise the Indian influence in the heroine's so gentle and so tender nature, in the candour of the characters and also in some poetic comparisons, in some gracious compliments strewn here and there in the narrative.[19] We can however note that the narrative is in itself of a precision and sobriety pretty rare in Indian narrators.

English influence can also be noted in *The Diary of Mademoiselle D'Arvers*. It is betrayed in the detailing of family occupations, in the intimate charm of the home.

This work that takes us from idyll to drama, from drama to idyll, by turns, this work interests us by its admirable ingenious character. With the impressionability of the women of her race, Toru Dutt retraces, in a natural and touching language, all that is felt by Marguerite d'Arvers, from the naïve joy of the adolescent, to the terrible emotions of the fiancée; from the domestic bliss of the wife and mother, till the sadness of the young woman who is about to die leaving behind her husband and son. In the first pages of the diary of Marguerite, it is very much a child of fifteen years, who with her pretty patter, lets us into her family affection, into her works of charity, into her rural joys. Then, under the weight of terrible ordeal, it is a woman who rises in all the brilliance of her devotion and who bears her sorrow on the

---

19. Note also as proof of Indian influence the following reflection of Marguerite d'Arvers about the Count of Plouarven: 'His colouring was of an almost feminine fairness, that denotes his high birth.' Since ancient times in India, the fairness of the skin was a sign of aristocracy; it was one of the traits that distinguished the conquering race of the Aryans from that of the native race of the Dasyous/ Dravidians.

cross in whose shadow she has been brought up. Toru Dutt knew well how to interpret the sentiments of a Breton Catholic girl. How pleasant it is for Marguerite d'Arvers to recall the convent where she grew up, the angelic nun whom she saw die and whose intercession she asks for in heaven! As a fiancée, she places her marriage under the protection of the Blessed Virgin. As a wife and soon a mother, she invokes Mary as the Mother of infant Jesus.

Many times, while reading Marguerite d'Arvers' narrative, who too seems a young girl from India transported to our Christian France, I felt I heard Toru herself as revealed to me by her letters and her father's letters. In her heroine, I found her ingenuous grace, the exquisite sensitivity of her so-loving heart, her faith so deep and so tender. In the paternal home of Mademoiselle D'Arvers, I recognized that of our young Hindu girl. Seeing Marguerite with her parents, it seems to be really Toru amidst her mother and father.

I also noted the funeral thought which slowly appears in the diary of Marguerite d'Arvers. First, the young girl, quite in the illusions of the sixteenth year, does not understand that one might want to die. All the forces of her bright youth fight against this thought: 'Poor Sister!' she says, talking about the dying Sister Véronique. 'She is so young! She is only twenty-six years old! It is too early to die! To leave this beautiful world where we enjoy the blessings of our Lord . . . Sister Véronique was happy to die! I could not understand it.'

'If there are bitter days, there are sweet ones too!'

'And till now, I have had no suffering; the world is so beautiful!'

But the illusions break, life appears as it really is to Marguerite: a trial meant to make us worthy of the eternal life. After the moral distress comes the physical distress that Toru Dutt retraces with striking reality, and the idea of death in the last part of the work, with a persistence that betrays the preoccupations of the author and the progress of her illness. However the idea of death is always accompanied by the idea of eternity, and the ray of immortality that Marguerite d'Arvers sees shining at the death bed of Sister Véronique, shines also at her own death bed, as it did at that of Toru Dutt's.

If in Marguerite d'Arvers we find the sentiments, character and the premature death of Toru Dutt, the resemblance stops there. Our young Hindu did not see the storm swoop down on her that broke over the life of Marguerite. Toru Dutt, having died a young girl, did not experience either the conjugal love or the maternal love that she so delightfully made her heroine express, and that she only knew with the prescience of her heart. Her mother and father remain alone to mourn for her and to await, with the unshakeable firmness of their faith, the moment of seeing her in eternity. But the memory of her life does not belong only to her parents; the fame of her works has entered into the heritage of the literary world. England and India claim this young glory, and I like to say to myself that France as well, will retain the memory of this young foreigner who, at the very moment our country was humiliated, wanted to belong to it as much as through language, as with the heart.

August 1878, Paris   Clarisse Bader

Today is my birthday. I am fifteen years old. In five years' time I will be twenty. How time flies. My dear mother is all worked up, as there is going to be a grand dinner in my honour at our home! I have just left the convent where I spent such happy years. I have been here for the past two days. All the sisters presented me with a gift each. They were really sad to see me leave forever with my dear father, especially Sister Véronique; she prayed with me for a long while in front of the altar, and then she gave me a small silver cross.

'It will bring you good luck, my dear,' she said as she tied it around my neck with a black ribbon. 'This cross has consoled me in my moments of anguish and it will console you as well when you need it. Think always of Him who died on the Cross; I know the softness of your heart, the confidence that you have in the promises of our God. He will protect you against all evil, and He will bless you.'

I wept on leaving her, for she had really been like an elder sister to me during my entire stay in the convent. My father was waiting in the hall, and together we left this peaceful sojourn. I am so happy to see my dear father again! I kissed him so many times before we reached home. He laughed, all happy to see me.

'Here, my little one,' he said, 'you have become so tall and beautiful; your mother will not recognize you!'

'So you find me well then, my father?'

'Wonderful, dear!'

'Ah! You flatter me! My cheeks are a little too pink. Mademoiselle Lemoyne told me so, and I am a bit dark; she, she is all blond . . .'

'Yellow, like wheat,' said my father, smiling.

'Ah! It was Musset who wrote that.'

'What! You read Musset in the convent?'

'No. But Mademoiselle Bertha Frith, the Englishwoman, has a collection of French poetry, and she lent it to me.'

'Well, and this blonde woman?'

'Mademoiselle Lemoyne, my father!' I exclaimed. 'Yes, she is beautiful, and all white, with a mass of blond hair; but I prefer Sister Véronique, and I want to talk to you about her. She is younger than

Mademoiselle Lemoyne, I think, even though she looks more aged. She is so good! You see, father, whereas Mademoiselle smiled or laughed at my awkwardness or my inexperience (she could hardly help it as I was so gauche the first month), Sister Véronique helped me and told me how I should do such and such a thing. You see, the first month, I was sad because I missed you and mamma so much so that I only cried and prayed in my little room, and Sister Véronique realised it and took pity on me. Her father and her mother are both dead; she talked to me about them, and her brother who also died very young, and then of a ship's captain, her cousin, whose vessel sank. No one was saved, and her cousin too perished in that; so she took her vows.'

We talked in this vein all the way, and the next morning we arrived home. Mother was waiting for us at the door. I ran to hug her.

'Oh, mother!'

'My child!'

Father is very happy and content to have me home after such a long separation. It is he, seeing me in the kitchen with my mother, who told me to rest a while and not to do anything.

'For it is your birthday,' he added.

Mamma and I were in the kitchen to prepare some fine dishes. It is difficult to get good cooks in the locality. There are going to be a lot of people this evening at our place. The Countess of Plouarven is going to come with her two sons. The Count, the elder son, is very young, and Thérèse told me yesterday evening that he was 'as handsome as a prince'. We were childhood friends, but I hadn't seen him since I'd left for the convent, more than four years ago. Children forget fast.

My mother has just left me to go and dress up, as it is almost six o'clock and we dine at seven. She found me, hair undone, sitting in front of the table.

'What are you doing my little one?' she asked, running her hands over my hair. 'Don't waste any more time. In fact, Marguerite, to arrange all that hair, you need two full hours.'

And she lifted the black mass of hair in her hands, proud of the abundance of her daughter's hair. She kissed me on the forehead.

'Make yourself beautiful; your father likes to see you with blue ribbons.'

'And in white muslin, doesn't he?'

'Yes, little one.'

And kissing me once again, she left the room. Ah! There goes the clock: six-thirty. I must stop now.

21 August 1860

Oh! I was so happy last evening. Everyone congratulated me, and champagne was drunk to my health. But one must begin at the beginning. When I entered the hall, Madame Goserelle and her daughter were already there. They were talking to my mother. My father whispered in my ears that I was as beautiful as the flower that I was named after. Mademoiselle Goserelle, seeing me, took my hand with kindness.

'Ah! Here's the little one', she said. 'She has grown, hasn't she mother?'

Mademoiselle Euphonie Goserelle is the beauty of the village. She is older than me; I think she is twenty-six years old. She is tall, has hair of a rusty blond that seem to form a halo round her head, eyes of pale blue, but very lively; a long and fine nose, a large forehead, lips a bit too thin, and beautiful, regular teeth. She is always laughing; father says it is to show off her beautiful teeth, but I don't believe him; you cannot laugh without wanting to, and then father jests with me often. As I was talking to Mademoiselle Goserelle, the door opened and the Countess of Plouarven and her younger son Gaston, were announced. My mother received them and seated the Countess on the sofa.

'And Marguerite?' asked Madame de Plouarven, smiling. 'Where is she?'

My mother signaled to me to come over, and I approached them. The countess took hold of both my hands, made me sit next to her, and looked at me for a long time.

'You are very beautiful and kind, my child.' And she passed her lips over my forehead. 'You see', she continued playfully, 'you used to come so often to the chateau, to play with Dunois and Gaston that

I've got used to talking to you with the familiar 'tu', and I've got used to thinking of you as my child. You will not be able to recognise Dunois, I suppose?'

'No, I don't think so; I was just a child then.'

'And what are you now, my girl?' she continued with her charming smile. 'You are just fifteen years really. Dunois is twenty-three.'

And as the door reopened: 'Ah! There he is; isn't he handsome?' she asked with maternal pride.

'Yes.'

That escaped me unwittingly, as it was the truth. He is in fact handsome. He is tall, but some may find him thin; his black hair is curled and falls to his neck. His black eyes are deep and wide, his upper lip covered with a budding black moustache is perfectly modeled; his chin has a touch of severity. His colouring is almost femininely white, which denotes his high birth. His mother signaled to him to come over to her.

'See Dunois, this is Marguerite! Hasn't she grown?'

He bowed low to me. The countess made him sit next to her.

'Shake hands, my children,' she said smilingly. 'You used to hug before without any fuss.'

It made me turn red. She took my hand and put it in the hand of the count, who smiled and said, 'Oh, mother! She is innocent and tender like an angel, and does not know that Mademoiselle Goserelle is looking at us!'

'Well, let her look!' said the countess smilingly. 'Am I doing something improper?'

And as I removed my hand, she cried out again gaily and kissed me on the forehead; and then running her hands over my hair and turning to her son, she asked, 'You find her beautiful, don't you?'

'Ah, yes, my mother!' he said smilingly, 'but not more so than you . . .'

22 August

This morning, Papa and I went to the woods; we met the count and his brother there. I was eating blackberries and wild berries whose juice had coloured my lips. Suddenly, we heard the sound of hooves, and the count and his brother appeared before us. I would have liked to run away as, with my hair disheveled and my violet lips, I was not fit to be seen. Papa held me by the arm. His eyes shone with mischief.

'There, Dunois, you have a wild Bretonne,' he said laughingly.

'More a wood nymph, General,' replied the count, with a friendly smile.

That made me blush. Did he mean that I was beautiful in this disorderly state? We talked until noon, and then we returned home. The count asked me when I would come to visit his mother.

'Not before a fortnight,' replied my father. 'You see, Dunois,' he added, placing his hand on my shoulder, 'I haven't had her for so long that I can't bear to have her out of my sight even for a moment. But, she will go to the castle in two or three weeks, if madame, your mother, wishes to have her.'

The count seemed happy with this promise. He assured us that the countess would always be willing to receive me.

23 August

This morning, I went to see all the old people in the village. One family interests me a lot. There is only the old father, who is called André Corraine, his wife Michelle and the daughter Jeannette, a beautiful person, kind and active, sixteen years old. Pitiable people! They are in great poverty. The daughter does her best to earn the daily bread, but that is not enough for the three of them. They hardly grumble, and don't talk of their distress to anyone; but despite their reserve, I can well see what is happening. I will talk about it to the wonderful countess, for I think she is looking for a good chamber maid.

24 August

This morning I was seated at the window. It was wonderful weather, the sky was so clear, without any clouds! I thought of the goodness of the Lord towards us sinners. Glancing at the fountain, I spotted a sparrow quenching its thirst there. Each time he drank, he lifted his head to the sky as if to thank his Creator, the father of all goodness. Lord, give me a heart sensitive to your good deeds and to your mercy! I visited mother Grestine today. She is the oldest woman in the village; and then I went to the Corraine's place. I found Jeannette boiling some meager soup; I threw in a piece of bacon and a cauliflower which I had in my box. I cooked a dozen potatoes under the ashes. The whole made a good meal for the poor people. The father and the mother, seeing me do all this, wanted to stop me, but I told them not to interfere. Jeannette followed me till the small compound; she wanted to thank me, but I closed her mouth with a kiss. Her eyes were full of tears; mine too for that matter, despite all my efforts.

I returned singing a country air, when I heard papa calling out to me.

'At last, there you are, my little one,' he said coming out of the hall. 'I was wondering what had become of you.'

'Were you searching for me, papa? I am very sorry.'

'Come in then,' he said. 'Here's Louis, who has been here for an hour, and no one in the house to talk to him, but me.'

My father then introduced me to a young officer whom I had never seen before.

'This is my daughter, Louis,' said my father. 'My only child.'

The officer gave me his hand with such a frank smile and such a friendly look that I immediately felt at ease.

'You don't remember him, do you, Marguerite?' asked my father.

'No,' I replied shaking my head.

'Ah! You were so young then, both of you!'

Louis is hardly twenty years old. A tanned face, with a chest like Hercules, hair brown and thick: there's his portrait in a few words. His brown eyes, bold and limpid, are full of softness and sincerity. His lips have sometimes an expression of sorrow, especially when he talks of his mother; but when they laugh, his whole face lights up. My father put his hand on my shoulder.

'Careful!' he said in a mocking and pedantic tone. 'You see before you the famous Captain Louis Lefèvere, of the 22nd Light Cavalry, who has just come from Algeria. He will remain awhile here. Get a room ready for him, little one; but first, run and tell your mother that Louis has arrived. I could not find her, or else I would have given her the good news myself.'

I found my mother in the kitchen garden, tending to her peas and her beans.

'Louis Lefèvere is here, mother.' I said to her.

She turned around briskly.

'What are you saying?' she exclaimed. 'Come here and let me hug you for the good news, little one.'

She gave me a kiss, and then went towards the house holding me by my hand.

'Oh, Henry,' she told my father. 'Why didn't you let me know earlier?'

'Because I didn't find you anywhere, my dear,' replied my father, lifting his eyes from a new rifle he was showing to Louis.

'My dear Louis, I am so happy to see you.'

She went towards the captain and kissed him on the forehead. He was moved; his lips trembled, and his eyes veiled over. Papa pulled me to his side; I saw that his eyes too were damp. I didn't understand anything then. But I know all now. Louis was an orphan at seventeen, his mother having died two days after his father, who belonged to the same regiment as my father. The young man had left for Africa, overwhelmed with grief, almost mad. He loved them so much. It was the last time my parents had seen him . . . But let us finish my story.

'And you were always well, Louis?' continued my mother.

'Not always; I had fever three days after my departure, and it lasted more than a month. But at present,' he added smilingly, 'I have the best health in the world.'

After dinner, papa left Louis in my charge, saying:

'Now, Marguerite, show all your protégés to Louis; I am going to write my letters and your mother will prepare the room.'

I escorted my guest to the garden and showed him my rabbits. He took one in his arms to caress it, but the mischievous one bit his finger. I saw him putting the animal gently down on the lawn, as if nothing had happened, but soon I saw a red thread flowing from his finger.

'Did the animal bite you?' I asked.

He smiled, 'Ah, it is nothing.'

But I insisted, and then he showed me the mark of four little teeth. I bandaged his finger.

'I am so angry,' I said. 'But you are not in great pain, are you?'

'Not at all,' he replied.

And then more softly, he added, 'How you remind me of my mother!'

I didn't say anything.

'Have you seen her?' he asked in the same voice.

'I think so, but I don't remember it.'

We went and sat down in the shade of an old oak tree.

'Were you very ill in Africa?'

'There was no hope of saving me; there was no dear one close to my bed to console me. It was a month after the death of my parents; a friend looked after me. I saw my mother many times during my delirium. I saw her white as marble, but with a soft smile which lit up her face. She took my hands, she put her lips on my burning forehead, and then I got up relieved physically, but desolate that I was going to take longer to join her.'

He fell silent, and looked at the fields all dreamy.

I cried. Suddenly, he turned his head.

'Are your tears flowing for me?' he asked.

'You have suffered so much!' I replied to him.

After a silence, he said in his natural voice, 'Well, show me your father's old horse.'

25 August

This morning, very early, I was feeding the hens and the ducks before breakfast. Louis joined me.

'You are an early riser today; but so am I,' he said.

'Yes, but how is your finger?'

'Very well, I think, even if I haven't seen it this morning.'

'You haven't removed the bandages?' I asked in astonishment.

'No, it was you who put them on, and it will be you who will remove them.'

I did as he desired. Thérèse, the old nurse, came in at that moment.

'What is wrong with the Captain, mademoiselle?' she asked.

'My rabbit bit his finger, Thérèse.'

'Only that? Ah! my child, he has been more deeply hurt, I think.'

And she went away. Louis bent down a little to look at me; his look intrigued me.

'She is my mother's nurse,' I said. 'But have you never been hurt?'

'Three times,' he replied after a pause.

'Seriously?'

'I only count the serious wounds that I have received.'

After breakfast, we all went to the woods. Papa and mamma returned to the house before us. As Louis and I were sitting on the edge of the small river, Louis said, looking at the path, 'Someone is coming.'

I turned my head.

'It is the count,' I said.

Louis frowned.

'What count? What is his name?'

'The count of Plouarven.'

'Do you know him?'

'Yes, his mother was in the same convent as mine.'

The count reached us and greeted me, then, turning towards Louis, he held his hand out to him.

'I have the honour of talking to Captain Lefèvre,' he said. 'My father belonged to the same regiment as you.'

Louis smiled.

'Really?' he replied in a good mood.

We began to talk.

'My mother is still expecting you,' said the count. 'When will we have the pleasure of seeing you at the castle?'

'After a fortnight perhaps.'

'I am happy that my uncle will be coming around the same time, otherwise I fear you would get bored in the castle.'

'Oh, no! I am sure not.'

'I believe you, one doesn't get bored when one has a good soul.'
'That is quite true, what you say,' replied Louis, who was throwing pebbles into the lake with a dreamy look.

We soon got up to return to the house. Before leaving us, the count told Louis, 'I hope to see you soon. My uncle would be delighted to make your acquaintance.'

'Thank you,' replied Louis, all happy. And the count went away.

29 August

Louis left this morning. We were very sad about it. Mamma hugged him and could not contain her tears; she made him promise ten times that he would return soon. Papa and I accompanied him some part of the way. We were all silent, for saying 'goodbye' to a friend, even if it is followed by 'see you soon', is always sad. At the corner by the church, he left us.

'You will not forget me?' he asked, shaking my hand.

'Oh! no. You may believe it.'

'And I,' he continued in a lowered voice, 'I will never forget you, even if I never see you again.'

'But we will see each other again, and you will return!' I replied, as he talked a little sadly.

'And you will be happy to see me?'

'Happy to see you. What a question! We will be very happy to see you again, won't we, my father?'

'Yes, my child,' said my father looking at Louis, and letting out a little sigh.

Louis climbed on his horse, and galloped away. Before disappearing into the woods, he turned and waved his hat. Papa took my face in his hands and looked a long time at me. How much he loves me, father! His eyes had become moist.

'My little innocent, flower of the fields,' he said kissing me softly on the forehead.

We returned towards the house.

'Come on,' said my father. 'We should not get sad. He will come back, I hope.'

'I hope so too,' I would have loved to have him remain a little while longer. His going away leaves a vacuum in our midst.

'Your mother is pained to see him leave; she loves that boy a lot, and I, I have a great affection for him. And you, Marguerite?'

'Me too, my father.'

The house is rather sad without Louis. Even though he had just spent a few days only with us, his departure makes us feel as if he were one of the family. The countess made a visit to us this evening. She came to request mamma and papa to accompany me to the castle; but they couldn't do so. I would have liked them to have accepted the invitation. The countess then said that she was in dire need of a chamber maid. So I spoke to her about Jeannette Corraine. She was willing to see her, and I promised her that I would tell Jeannette to go to the castle. She was touched to tears when I recounted to her the extreme poverty of the Corraines, and the devotion of their daughter. I have a strong hope that they will take Jeannette as a chamber maid.

'You have hardly been here a month in our midst, and you already know all the poor people,' said the countess, very surprised and happy. 'You are their guardian angel, it seems.'

4 September

This morning, Papa received a letter from Louis. He is at present in Paris, but he will be leaving shortly for Algeria. He will return in December and 'then,' he wrote, 'I hope to see you all. I will never be able to forget all the care you and madame d'Arvers have taken of my parents and me. I can never be thankful enough for all the goodness that you have shown during my days of sorrow. Pray that the God of the heavens protects you from all evil, you and your loved ones! Do not forget me during my voyages; but it would be redundant to tell you so, as you take the place of my father, and madame d'Arvers that of my mother, and I know that you will always have a place in a corner of your heart for—Louis Lefèvre.'

I went with the countess today to see Jeannette Corraine. Gaston accompanied us. The countess is happy with the girl, and she engaged her on the spot. Jeannette was very happy. She kissed my hands; she cried, and her tears moved me. I told her to calm down; her mother and her father blessed me loudly. Jeannette will go tomorrow to the castle. While coming back, Gaston said, 'You are very kind.'

'No, I want to be so, but I am not.'

'But what would the poor girl have done without you?' he exclaimed.

'Ah! God would hardly have abandoned her. He likes his creatures, he calls them his children—and a father will hardly neglect his children.'

There was a silence.

'The girl is very pretty,' carried on Gaston.

'I am happy that you think like me; her big eyes, aren't they beautiful? Blue like a summer sky.'

'Does this sentence come from your heart?'

'What do you mean?' I replied, lifting my eyes to meet his full of mischief. He smiled.

'It does not matter what I mean.'

And on that note we went our ways, as we were by then close to the compound of our garden.

5 September

Tomorrow I leave for the castle. I was busy the whole morning, packing. The bell strikes eight o'clock; I've left the window open; the shining stars look at me, and the silvery moon divides my room into light and shade. All is quiet; not a sound, not the slightest breath of wind. I became all dreamy. The moon made me think of Sister Véronique of my convent; she too is chaste and beautiful and pale, like the star of the night. Far from the noise of the world, she leads a life of calm and piety. How good she is! She loves me a lot, and that makes me happy, for being loved by such a saintly and good person is a kind of happiness. I still wear round my neck the crucifix that she gave me.

7 September

Château de Plouarven. Here I am finally, at the old castle; I like this place. The castle has an air of grandeur, but there is something gloomy about it that makes me sad and pensive despite myself when I am all alone. But I am well settled in, and everything is made comfortable and agreeable for me. Yesterday, at five in the evening, the count and his brother came to take me; the big family carriage followed them. I said that I would prefer to go on foot. Papa burst into laughter.

'Does the carriage scare you, my little one? Would you perhaps be scared of falling?'

The count smiled.

'I am of your opinion, mademoiselle,' he said.

I could not stop some tears from brimming to my eyes, despite my best efforts, when I kissed my mother.

'Come on', she said in a low voice, 'don't cry. Won't I see you often, and isn't all this for your good?'

We took the path through the woods, as it is the most shady. The count walked on my left, and his brother on my right. We talked of Louis; the count wanted to know his story. I asked Gaston if their mother was happy with Jeannette. He replied that she didn't stop talking of her dedication and her good manners. The count made me admire the countryside rolling out in front of us. The bleak and sad castle was at that moment bathed in the bright red rays of the setting sun; a mountain covered with bramble, brushwood, and other kinds of grasses could be seen behind the big edifice. We crossed a big meadow; all around were fields of barley and oats thriving in the sun. Autumn has not yet started to shed her golden rays on the trees. Summer is in all her glory. Everything was quiet, except for some birds, and the river flowing at the foot of the mountain. The countess was waiting for us under the gothic vault. She embraced me with affection, and led me to the drawing room.

'I am so happy to see you here, my dear,' she said to me, and added, 'but, Dunois, why did you not bring her in the carriage?'

'Mademoiselle preferred to walk, and since her idea seemed the best to me too, I did not oppose it,' he replied with his charming smile.

'But you are tired, aren't you, my child?' asked the countess.

'Not at all. The walk did me good; the air is so fresh in the woods!'

Then she asked for news of my father and mother. She said that her brother had arrived, but that he had gone out. He was to return before dinner.

'I will show you your room, my child. You must rest a little before dinner.'

I followed her into the room which she called mine! A thousand perfumes of the fields and the soft fragrance of jasmine filled the room. Below, a magnificent garden stretched out. Far away, really far away, one could see a long blue line that shimmered in the sun: it was the sea. I was charmed; I ran to the countess. In my joy, I embraced her.

'What a beautiful room! You are so kind!'

She seemed happy.

'I will willingly give it to you forever, if it is possible,' she said smiling, yet pensive.

And then she added, 'Come on, Marguerite. Make yourself at home. If you finish dressing up before me, don't wait for me, but go down bravely to the drawing room. They will be happy to see you.'

With that she left me. When I found myself alone, I knelt down as usual in the alcove before the crucifix that was placed there. I thanked the Lord for all His goodness, and I prayed to Him to give me grace to be able to do all that is good. Oh God, forgive me all my sins, for they are innumerable! I got up and looked out of the window; then I put on my white muslin dress, with blue satin ribbons. My father likes to see me dressed like that. Then I went down. I was about to enter the drawing room when the door opened and a man came out. He was about fifty years old. His hair was turning gray, as well as his thick moustache. His eyes were small, but full of life. On seeing me, he came towards me, and shaking my hand he said gaily, 'I know you, mademoiselle, by hear-say. My sister has spoken to me of you; she is very fond of you, and my God, she is right. I am Colonel Desclée.'

He seemed to want to read my heart, for he looked at me, for a few minutes, with interest, and then said, 'Well, my little one, you please me.' He added, 'Let us go in.'

He led me to the drawing room, holding me by my hand. I am

very happy to make his acquaintance, for I had thought of him as a severe and hard man, but he is very likeable. We found the count and his brother in the drawing room whose windows open on to the terrace full of statues and rare and beautiful plants. The colonel, it seemed, had taken a liking to me. I was happy to see Jeannette and to learn that she was happy. She thanked me with one of her soft smiles, and a thankful look in her big blue eyes.

8 September

This morning, I went to see my mother and father. This is how it happened. At lunchtime, the colonel asked me whether I knew how to ride, and I replied no, I didn't.

He turned towards the count and exclaimed, 'My dear Dunois, why don't you teach her how to?'

The count welcomed the idea with pleasure.

'We will start today itself, if it is alright with you, mademoiselle, and we will go and see your mother . . .'

'Oh! That would be charming, but . . .'

'No *buts*,' interrupted the colonel gaily.

'But,' I repeated, 'Perhaps you may not have a horse docile enough for me to mount.'

'Yes, we do,' replied the count. 'My mother bought a white mare just about a year ago, as gentle as a sheep.'

'My sister bought it for the future countess, didn't you, my sister?' said the colonel with a sly grin.

The countess smiled, and her son went to make the arrangements. Gaston said that he could not accompany us as he had other work to do. After dinner the horses were brought to the door. The count's horse, called Saladdin, is shiny black in colour, with not a single white hair, and is huge, with a magnificent chest. At the sound of his master's voice, he pricked his ears and neighed with joy. The mare meant for me was as white as snow, with a flying, silvery mane. She is really as gentle as a sheep. The mare next to Saladdin—one looks all force and grandeur, and the other all beauty and gentleness. I caressed Fatima, and she seemed to make out that I like horses, because she neighed softly with pleasure and licked my hands. The count held the stirrup, and he jumped lightly on to his horse. The countess smilingly wished us a safe journey.

'Take care Dunois,' she said to her son, 'that no misadventure happens to Marguerite'.

'Don't worry about anything, mother,' replied the count gaily.

He asked me whether I was comfortable in my saddle.

'Perfectly fine,' I replied.

He gave me a beautiful whip, encrusted with silver.

The colonel exclaimed, 'But you mount very well, little one!'

I smiled. We trotted off, but after a few minutes, we galloped. The count rode close to me in case of any accident. The morning was so fresh, the sky so blue, and I was so happy! At our garden gate, I jumped lightly from my horse, without help, and ran to embrace my father, who was walking about at the threshold.

'Well, well,' he said all delighted. 'Look at you, on top of a horse, but that is wonderful! Just now seeing an Amazon with two riders coming towards me I said to myself, "There is Mademoiselle Goserelle who is coming with her escorts."'

He was truly delighted to see me. Mamma ran to receive the count and his uncle, and seemed as happy to know that I had come on a horse. At the end of an hour, we returned to the castle.

9 September

This afternoon, we were on the banks of the river. The count wanted to go on a boat and we all joyfully agreed. The count, his brother and I sailed gaily between the two banks of bramble and eglantine. The countryside was so gentle and charming! In the distance we could see, over the top of the trees, the tall tower of the castle. Everything was quiet around us; we could only hear our own voices. Here and there a goldfish or an azure fish showed up on the surface, and then rushed down like an arrow. I admired the roses briefly glimpsed between the bushes; I was in ecstasy in front of a beautiful rose white as snow. The count jumped to the ground and plucked it. The bank was steep, and he almost fell, and I could not hold back a cry. Gaston, who was dreamily looking at the stream jumped up, but the count had regained his balance and he entered the boat with the rose in hand.

'How pale you are!' he said offering the flower to me. 'Are you not feeling well?'

'No, I was scared seeing you slip, that is all.'

'But I know how to swim,' replied Dunois. 'Get back your rosy cheeks mademoiselle, and don't look as white as this flower,' he added smilingly.

We returned to the castle, and Gaston recounted to his mother all our adventures. The countess hearing that I had got scared, embraced me tenderly and called me 'her daughter'.

10 September

This evening we dined on the terrace; it was hot inside the house. As when the sun was setting against a purple sea, the countess and her brother returned home. The long dusk of the evening invited us to remain outside. After a few minutes, Gaston looked at his watch and got up to leave. The count frowned slightly, and wanted to say something to him, but Gaston had already moved away. I looked at the goldfish in the fountain basin. As for the count, he stood next to me, all dreamy. The small fish frolicked in the clear water.

'It's charming!' I exclaimed. 'How beautiful it is!'

'It is indeed beautiful, your face was reflected in the water,' he said smiling.

'That is not it,' I said all taken aback. 'I was looking at the small fish which are charming to look at.'

'And I was looking at the silhouette, beautiful and charming, of your face.'

That made me blush more than ever. His words gave me so much pleasure! His sonorous voice with just a slight tone of gaiety, is harmonious to hear, like the sound of the waves against the rocks. We soon went in as night had fallen. The countess begged me to sing a country song. As I finished doing so, the colonel congratulated me.

'You sing like a nightingale of the rose woods, my dear,' he said. 'Come on Dunois, it is your turn now; sing us a song.'

The count took his violin, an instrument he plays to perfection, and he started singing a song whose words were by Victor Hugo. His baritone voice seemed to fill the room.

'S'il est un charmant gazon
Que le ciel arrose . . . '
(If there is a charming lawn
That the heaven does spray upon . . .)

After he finished this piece, the colonel remarked, 'That's good my child; I think you have made a lot of progress since I heard you sing last year.'

Gaston had returned. He was asked to sing, but he excused himself. At eleven o'clock we parted. In my room, I knelt down at the foot of the cross in the alcove. May God forgive me my trespasses and guide my wandering footsteps. I am your servant, O my Lord, have pity on me. I opened the window and I looked out. The moon lit up the top of the fir trees and the birches. Everything was so peaceful! I could hear only the dull booming of the sea against the rocks. I could catch a glimpse in the distance of the silvery crests of the waves. I was to return home tomorrow, but the countess didn't agree to that so I will be staying two more days.

11 September

The count and Gaston showed me all the nooks and crannies of the castle. We went up the tower, and there we sat on the bastion and saw the setting sun disappear in the distance into the blue waves of the ocean.

'This tower has its own legend,' said the count.

'Oh please tell me about it, I beg of you.'

Gaston walked about. The count spoke, 'One of my ancestors, named Henry de Plouarven, lived in this castle in I don't know which year of the twelfth century. He then had but one child, a girl sixteen years old, very beautiful, and of a sweet and gentle nature. She was the sole joy of Count Henry. He had a son, but he had left a few years earlier for the crusades. Well, one day in December, a horse rider came to the castle, in the mist. People hastened to offer him shelter and hospitality for it was very cold outside. The rider was covered in snow. Catherine, that was the name of the count's daughter, came to remove the shoulder belt of the young man, as that was the custom those days. The count invited his guest to the table. He was a man about twenty-five years of age, his armour was black, only the plume of his helmet was white, white as the snow. He was tall, his curly hair fell on his temples, hair that was ebony black, and half hid a scar on his forehead. This scar, and his thick and black moustache, showed up his virile beauty. He didn't tire of looking at the young girl with his black, pensive eyes. The young girl loved him from the first moment. Her clear, blue eyes furtively stared fixedly at the noble face of the horseman. Her gentle and innocent body coloured up at the smallest compliment he paid her. The count pressed him to stay on a day or two more in the castle. While leaving, the rider gave a white rose as a souvenir to Catherine. He wished her 'good bye' and not 'au revoir'. Catherine climbed up this tower to see him as long as she could. She saw his plume flying, his beloved figure becoming smaller and smaller, and then disappear altogether. She went into the tower and slept on his bed. Her father, not seeing her, came in search of her in the evening. He entered the tower. The moon illuminated the room with a pale, silvery light coming in through the bars of the Venetian blinds. The count saw the young girl sleeping on the bed, paler than the flower she was holding in her hand. In the moonlight, her blonde hair resembled a halo around her head. The count wanted to wake her up but she was dead. It is said,' continued Dunois, 'that if you come to the tower any night in December, when there is moonlight, you can see the same thing that Count Henry saw that night.'

It was already dark, and the wind began to shake the leaves.

'But you are cold!' exclaimed the count, covering me with a coat. 'Your hands are frozen. Let us go down.'

And we went down.

12 September

This morning the colonel left for Paris. He promised his sister that he would be back before 20 November, the feast day of the count. At the threshold he shook my hand and then kissed me on the forehead saying, 'Come, come, my little one, you should not say no to an old scar-face like myself. With M. Dunois, I admit it would be different, wouldn't it?'

And he began to laugh. It made me blush. I am leaving tomorrow. Oh! To be close to my mother and father, it makes me so happy just to think of it! The countess begged me to come to the castle in November for the feast day of the count, who himself insisted, saying with his gracious smile, 'You will come, won't you? You see, we can't do without you, can we, mother?'

'That goes without saying, my son. You will come won't you, my dear Marguerite?'

I promised them I would.

13 September

Here I am in my own small room with its window overlooking the orchard and my bed with white curtains, and my small table on which I write my diary. The count and his brother accompanied me home. Papa was waiting at the door. I jumped at his neck, and as I hugged him, 'People would think that you had been away a year instead of a week,' he said laughing, but his eyes were moist.

Mamma was in her room. I ran to find her there. She hugged me saying all surprised:

'But I thought that you were returning this evening. Who accompanied you?'

'The count and Gaston.'

Mamma came down to the drawing room and I followed her. The count handed over a letter from his mother to her and begged her, as well as my father, to come to the castle on his feast day. She thanked him and accepted his invitation. As soon as the count and his brother had left, I ran to see my 'ménagerie' as my father calls it. The rabbits reminded me of Louis. At dinner, I asked my father if he had any news of Louis.

'This very morning I received a letter from him,' he replied, looking at my mother.

'He is not ill, is he?' I asked.

'No.'

'Where is he?'

'In Corsica.'

'Really! And how does he find the country? Read me his letter then, father.'

My father read a few lines, and then he stopped.

'He only talks of his stay here with us, and the happy days he spent at our place.'

He folded the letter and kept it back in his pocket. We went to sleep very late; we had so much to talk about!

14 September

The count came yesterday to enquire whether I wasn't tired after the long walk. Mamma showed him some exotic plants that she had lately got from Paris. He asked my mother news of Louis.

'I would be delighted to meet him again,' he said. 'A braver young man cannot be found. His frank open look and his sincere smile made me take him in affection,' he added smilingly.

'He will be visiting us in October.'

'Really! That makes me very happy, for I hope to introduce him then to my mother.'

My mother told him the whole story of Louis. The count listened to her attentively, his handsome face pensive, his big black eyes fixed on my mother.

'Poor young man!' he said at last. 'He has suffered a lot. His sad story makes me like him more than ever. And he is a captain, a man who seems so young!'

'He is hardly twenty years old; he is the youngest captain in his regiment,' replied my mother, so proud of her protégé.

The count took leave of us a few minutes later.

17 September

Oh! What a beautiful horse my Austerlitz is! My dear father! As soon as he saw that I liked to ride, he ordered a magnificent chestnut-coloured horse with a flying mane from Paris. The superb animal is as docile as a lamb, and seemed to recognize me as soon as he saw me. He arrived yesterday, and today we went all over the countryside. How fast he gallops; like the wind! My father and I met the count who didn't stop praising Austerlitz.

'I thought I saw Diana returning from her hunt!' he told me.

18 September

I received a letter from Sister Véronique today. She is ill, very ill, and she wants to see me as soon as possible. The letter, short though it was, was full of a spirit at peace with her God. Poor sister! She is so young! She is only twenty-six years old! It is too early to die, to leave this beautiful world where we enjoy the bounties of our Lord. My father gave me permission to go and see her, and my mother cried on reading the letter. I leave at ten o'clock after breakfast.

21 September

I reached the convent of Mater Dolorosa on the evening of the 18. I entered the room of the sick person. She was lying in her bed, and on seeing me she smiled, and made a sign to me to approach her. I knelt down at her bedside; she embraced me. How pale she was! She was holding a small ivory crucifix in her hand. I sobbed.

'Poor Marguerite! You really liked me then?' she said softly, brushing her hand over my head. 'Do not cry, my child. I will be so happy, up in heaven! We will recognise each other there. This world is full of sorrow and afflictions, but close to our Father, "there will be no longer any mourning, or tears, or work, and God will wipe away all the tears from our eyes".'

She was silent, her eyes fixed on the symbol of suffering of our Saviour. She spoke again.

'Marguerite, you see this crucifix, it has consoled me so many times! I want it to be with me in my coffin.'

And as my tears flowed more and more, she added, 'I am happy to leave this world; I have suffered a lot in it. I am going to join my father and mother, and also Bernard.'

I remained in the room the whole night. Sister Dorcas kept vigil as well. Sister Véronique was so happy to die! I could not understand it.

S'il est des jours amers, il en est de si doux!
(If there are bitter days, there are sweet ones too!)

And till now, I have had no suffering, the world is so beautiful! In the morning, she called me.

'Are you there, Marguerite?'

'Yes.'

'Come closer, so that I can embrace you.'

I went closer to her and I held her white hands, already so cold, in mine.

'Sister Claire', she said to the sister who was close to her bedside. 'Open the windows so that I can see the sun once more.'

The sister did so. The brilliant light of the morning sun filled the small room; the feeble night light flickered and died out. Sister Véronique kept looking at the sun; her pale face glowed in the light.

'I will soon see a more glorious day, where the sun of justice shall rise, whose rays will carry health.'

She seemed to be praying, her hands were together. Then she said to Sister Claire:

'My sister, I want to see Father Augustin.'

The sister went out. Véronique took my hand in hers.

'Marguerite, forgive me all that I may have done to hurt you.'

'But you had nothing but kindness to give to me. It is me on the contrary, who needs to be forgiven,' I said crying.

The Father entered, knelt down and prayed next to the dying woman. A half hour passed by. She could hardly breathe, her eyes were shut. The priest stopped for a moment. She opened her eyes, her lips murmured, 'Jesus, my saviour', and her spirit left her corporal abode in peace. The priest got up.

'Our sister has gone to her rest. May God take her soul,' he said in a low voice.

I attended the funeral. I saw her in her coffin, her crossed hands were holding the crucifix, her pale face was illuminated with a strange light, her lips were smiling, she seemed to be sleeping rather than dead, and she was dressed all in white. My tears flowed but gently. It seemed to me that heavenly angels were in the room and were looking after the saintly dead. Each of the sisters placed her tribute on the coffin, and I placed a lily on the coffin that I had plucked that very morning. White candles lit up the cortège. She was placed in the vault of the chapel, and we prayed. I returned home after the ceremony. Sister Véronique was, like I had already said, an elder sister to me. In the convent, she was my companion and my teacher. I feel that I can still hear her gentle voice repeating the lines of the Gospel. She seemed to be a heavenly angel, and the Earth did not deserve her. She had suffered a lot in this world. The Lord, in his goodness, had taken her to him to intone his praises till eternity.

23 September

Today, in the morning, I went to see old Corraine and his old wife. Nearing the cottage I saw someone coming out of it. It was Gaston. I was very happy to see him concerned about the welfare of the poor, and I told him so. He blushed and asked me news of my mother and father, and then went away. I found Jeannette in the room; it surprised me and pleased me at the same time. The old people were talking about Gaston. Jeannette hurried to offer me a chair. I noticed that since Jeannette joined service in the castle, their situation had slowly improved. As old Corraine again started to thank me, I got up.

'If you thank me so many times, I will be forced to leave,' I told him with a smile and he kept quiet. After a long visit, I left them.

24 September

This morning, my father and I went for a walk very early before breakfast. The earth was covered with shimmering clear dew. Coming out of the dark forest, we suddenly found ourselves in the plains, lit up by the rising sun, and we climbed the hill that overlooks this plain. At the bottom, we saw the village, our white house with its compound, and clearly etched against the iridescent sky, the tall tower of castle Plouarven. Beyond that we could catch sight of the sea, making a thousand silvery and gold stars shimmer under the first rays of the sun. We returned home at breakfast time. Mamma was waiting for us at the threshold, and she gave a letter to Papa. 'From Louis', she said. He put it in his pocket, which surprised me a little, for normally he reads Louis' letters on the spot. But I was hungry and I hurried to take my place at the table.

25 September

The count came to see us. He requested my mother to allow me to go to the castle to help the countess with the preparations for the feast. During his visit Madame Goserelle and her daughter too came over. The count asked whether I rode everyday.

'But of course I do,' I replied.

'Will you allow me to accompany you soon?'

'Definitely!'

Madame Goserelle exclaimed laughingly, 'Ah! Monsieur le Comte, that is not very nice. When I come over, you are leaving.'

And as he didn't say anything she said again, 'It is a century since I saw you at our place.'

'Well, in fact, I have very little time for visits,' replied the count.

I went up to my room to wear my riding skirt. When I returned Dunois got up.

'Come on,' he said. 'Let us have an Epsom race.'

Papa went to change his shoes as he wanted to accompany us. Mademoiselle Goserelle came to see us off. The count helped me on to my saddle, and jumped on to his.

'It looks like a scene from a local legend,' said Mademoiselle Goserelle laughing. 'You are a very pretty horsewoman, Marguerite, you must accompany me on my horse rides.'

Papa soon joined us and we set off. Oh! How happy I was! We went on till the next village, and we returned after three hours of riding. The count left us at our door.

26 September

My mother and I visited the school-master and his wife. They live on the bank of the river. The husband earns some hundred and sixty francs per year, and his wife looks after the house and his children. They have three children: the eldest, a fat boy of eight, looks well and follows his father around everywhere. After him, there is a charming young girl of six, Hélène, who adores her brother Claude and looks upon him as her protector. The youngest is a small toddler of two, all rosy and laughing. We entered the house. Madame Valpoine welcomed us with joy. Her husband had left for school with young Claude, the father to teach, and the son to learn. Madame Valpoine wanted to show her small garden to my mother, I remained with the young one who laughed into my face, from his cradle. Soon Hélène ran into the room clapping her small hands.

'You have brought sweets and chocolate, haven't you?' She was already on my lap and was digging into my pocket and, finding what she was searching for there, gave me a kiss with her small rosy lips.

'I am going to eat the sweets,' she said all content.

'Not all of it, for you must keep half of it for Claude. He will be happy to find sweets after his books.'

She put aside the portion meant for Claude.

'My mother told me the other day not to eat too many sweets, because I would fall ill. Do you think so too?' she asked me.

'Definitely, if you eat too much you will be unwell and you do not want to be ill, I am sure.'

'Ah, no! Papa was ill the other day. He spent the whole day in bed, his eyes shut and he was shivering and trembling. Mamma said that it was fatigue, lack of rest. She did not say it was because of the sweets!'

We were there for about half an hour, and she was still chatting like a magpie when her father and Claude entered. The little one rushed down from my lap and went to give the sweets to Claude. M. Valpoine shook my hand; he loves his children with passion and likes those who show affection for them.

'Ah! Mademoiselle D'Arvers! you will spoil little Hélène,' he said. 'The little one likes you so much; you should hear her talk about you! You have a good heart, one can see that in the way you behave with children, and they are clever enough, the young ones, to recognise a friend.'

He took the baby from the cradle.

'Isn't he in good health?' he asked, hugging him.

He is indeed a pretty child with his chestnut curls and his big black eyes wide open. We returned home at the end of half an hour. Mamma said that the count, his mother and his brother went often to visit the school. It made me happy. The count is so good! He is interested in everything. Tomorrow we are going for a picnic given by the Goserelles.

28 September

Yesterday we went to the picnic at the Rose-woods. There were a lot of people already there when we arrived, but the count wasn't there, nor his mother or his brother. Mademoiselle Goserelle came to receive us with alacrity. She took me away.

'Everyone you see here is a friend of yours. There is no need to introduce you.'

One of her relatives, Monsieur Lance, a scholar, was talking to papa. On seeing me he asked, 'Is this your daughter, General?'

'Yes, she is,' replied my father.

He bowed deeply to me. He led us across the brush to a knoll where there were druid remains. He began to tell us in the tiniest detail all about the cult of the druids. He is very learned, and I tried to follow him. He seemed to be happy with my interest; Mademoiselle Goserelle joined us.

'My handsome cousin,' she said, laughing. 'Have mercy on this young girl, she is bored to death.'

'But of course not,' I replied. 'All this is very interesting.'

'You heard that, my beautiful cousin?' said Monsieur Lance.

We talked of a dozen things, when I heard the voice of the countess.

'Please excuse us this delay. Dunois had to attend to a lot of things.'

And then a voice that I recognised at once, asked, 'Has Mademoiselle D'Arvers come? And the General?'

He? He asking if I had come! It made me go pink with pleasure, and I no longer heard what Mademoiselle Goserelle was saying, nor Monsieur Lance. A hand was placed on my shoulder; I turned around, it was my father's. He seemed to listen to Mademoiselle Goserelle, pensively, and in a minute, the brush was moved apart and *he*, I mean the count, appeared.

'There you are Mademoiselle D'Arvers. I was searching for you everywhere.'

He noticed Mademoiselle Goserelle, and hands were shaken.

'Go and see the countess,' said my father.

I went away and the count followed me.

'And how is Austerlitz doing?'

'Very well, thank you.'

We arrived near the countess, who shook my hands and kissed my forehead.

'How beautiful you are my child,' she said to me. 'Isn't she, Dunois?' She looked up at him.

'It goes without saying, mother,' he replied smiling.

She seemed happy, and kissed his forehead.

'You are a good son, go on.'

She took my hand and we went to sit on the slope where everyone was gathered. Mademoiselle Goserelle sat next to me.

'You should be called Rose rather than Marguerite,' she said with a laugh. 'You have the same colour as the former.'

We seated ourselves around the white table cloth that had been spread out on the grass. Gaston was to my left, and Mademoiselle Goserelle to my right; she had the count to her right, Papa was next to the countess, and the scholar next to my mother. Gaston apologised for not having visited me more often.

'I had so much work!'

The day was joyful. In the evening the countess, the count, his brother, and us, all came back together. My father was a little thoughtful, and I heard my mother and him talking in their bedroom.

I soon went to sleep. Some time later, as if in a dream, a light sound. It was my mother. She bent over me and her lips were placed softly on my forehead. I flung my arms around her neck.

'Mother!' I murmured half asleep.

She went away and I went back into deep sleep. I dreamt dreams of happiness.

30 September

The last day of the month! I went to visit the tomb of Sister Véronique at the convent. Grass had covered the soil; the white marble cross bore these words:

'In memory of Sister Véronique, twenty-six years old.'
'Happy are you who cry, for you will be in joy.'

Alas! She had truly cried, the gentle saint! She had really suffered. May she be happy to see again all those she had cherished on earth! She used to love to talk so much of her family to me! She confided in me her anguish, her pain. She would speak with sadness, but also with hope, for she knew that she would soon be seeing her beloved ones. Gentle angel! Pray to God for me!

On returning, I met the count and his brother in the Avenue des Chênes. They were returning from fishing, their nets were well full. They accompanied me to our door, and there said good bye to me.

1 November

The count and his brother came today, and accompanied me in my horse ride across the plain. A shower took us by surprise; papa removed his bonnet to cover me.

'Am I scared of the rain?' I laughed, and put Austerlitz to gallop.

They did the same. The wind began to blow stronger, and the rain fell in big drops. I was drenched to the skin, my hair, undone by the wind, dripped shining pearls. When we reached home, we found my mother waiting for us at the door. The rain stopped after half an hour, and the count and his brother left when the sun reappeared.

4 November

The countess had come over this evening; she came purposely to request my mother to allow me to go help her with the preparations for the feast. My mother consented with pleasure. I have to go to the castle on the 16th at ten o' clock, and come back in the evening. Thérèse, our old servant, told me that all the people in the village, men, women, and children were getting ready for the 20th.

'He is a good boy, the count is,' she said. 'I remember the day that he was born as if it were yesterday. His father, the handsomest man one could ever see, gave gifts to each villager, man and woman. The day of baptism of the young heir, his father took him in his arms, and with his young and beautiful wife, he stood at the threshold, showing his son to all, one by one. My God! How many cheers went up! And to think that all this took place more than twenty years ago! Two years later, the count was killed in that battle field, and the whole village was in mourning, for the count was loved like a father, even if he was not more than twenty-three when he was killed. And the young countess fell ill, we thought that she would die, but the thought of leaving her two young ones all alone kept her going. Monsieur Dunois resembles his father with his noble and handsome features, he has the same black eyes, the same hair, but his brother, Monsieur Gaston, has the humorous nature of his father. May the good Lord and all the saints keep them safe! It is my prayer and that of the whole village.'

Thérèse is more than seventy years old. She sees me as a very small child, because she was my mother's nurse. Her old memories make me dream. I am not surprised that there was so much joy on the day the count was born.

6 November

My grand aunt who is in Paris sent me a beautiful dress of blue velvet with silver trimmings. Here is the letter that she wrote to me:

> Beautiful grand niece, your father gave me news of you. On opening his letter, I saw the portrait of the most beautiful girl in my acquaintance. I recognized you at first glance, even though

I haven't seen you for more than four years. I would really like
to see you, little one, but I am old, and the idea of travelling by
train frightens me. If you come to Paris with your father, do
not forget your old grand aunt.

Geneviève Hainault d'Arvers.

We went to see the Goserelles. Mademoiselle Euphonie led me to
her boudoir, and showed me some jewellery that she had received
from Paris. Above the mahogany table there is an oil portrait of a
young man. The sadness in his face struck me.

'Who is this young gentleman?' I asked Mademoiselle Goserelle.

'Ah! That is my cousin,' she said, and a soft sigh escaped her.

She leant against my shoulder.

'That one loved me. He died of consumption in Australia, poor
boy! I did not want to marry him; he didn't have a penny to his name,
and then he would have looked like my younger brother next to me.
No, truly, we were not made for each other.'

Then she went on to show me the portraits of her mother and her
late father. That story made me sad. We went for a horseback ride at
the edge of the lake after our visit.

A letter from Louis was awaiting my father; he put it in his pocket
without reading it.

'Go along then and read it, and tell us news of him, father,' I said.
'Why don't you read his letters like before?'

'Because there are, my curious one, some secrets that it is not fit
for you to know at present,' her replied, smiling, and gave me a little
tap on my cheek.

'What secrets could Louis then have? He is the frankest man in the
world.'

'He will tell you his secrets himself, one of these days, when he
will be here,' replied my father, laughing and kissing me on my cheeks.
'Go on, it is already late, rest a little before dinner.'

At dinner, Papa informed us that Louis would soon be coming to
see us. He will be here on the 18th.

'It is just before the feast,' I said.

'What feast? Ah! I remember; Dunois' feast,' said my father.

My mother is very happy at the idea of seeing Louis again, and to tell the truth, I am too.

9 November.

The count has not come to see us for some time now. I am afraid that he may be ill, but if he were, we would have known. The weather is a bit cool today. Papa and I had gone for a ride. I asked Papa if he remembered the late count.

'No, I had never seen him.'

We were on the hill.

'Look, Marguerite, don't you see someone on the platform of the castle?' he asked.

I looked, but saw no one.

'No, father, the sun is in my eyes.'

We turned back.

10 November

It is Sunday, and we had gone for Mass. We also went for the service in the afternoon. When we were about to go out, the count accosted us. I was so happy to see him as I was afraid that he had fallen ill. He greeted all of us and walked by my side. He was a little pale, and he was a little dreamy. I asked him if he had been ill.

'No, not really,' he replied smiling, 'but, last week, I had terrible headaches. You will come to see us on the 16th, don't forget. You brighten up the old castle.'

He left us at our doorway.

16 November

Today, at ten o' clock, the count came for me. He seems more gay and told us that he was feeling better, since we last saw him. His brother accompanied him. They said that their uncle had come. I talked little during our trip across the woods; I like to hear *his* voice. He talked of everything that could interest me. At the castle, the countess welcomed me with hugs and kisses, and the colonel shook my hand. The rooms were full of flowers, garlands, leaves and a thousand other things. I wanted to start the decorations on the spot, but the count did not agree, and neither did his mother.

'You must rest, Mademoiselle D'Arvers,' said Dunois.

After an hour of rest, we set to work. I had to decorate four portraits, of the late count, the countess, the count, and his brother. I placed a garland of everlasting flowers and pansies around the first two, and I tied them one to the other with an orange blossom chain. I framed the portraits of the count and his brother with red and white roses, with laurel leaves, and some fleur-de-lis. The countess admired all four of them. The colonel looked at the count's portrait for a long time, and said that he resembled his father a lot.

'Yes,' said the countess, 'but there is still a difference between them. Look at their eyes, and you will see that those of my Achille are softer than those of Dunois, which are a little sad and deep in my opinion. Moreover, Dunois' chin has something inflexible about it.'

'But also something male and clear, doesn't it?' retorted the colonel.

Below the late count's portrait was written: *Achille Dunois de Plouarven, at twenty years* and below the other : *Dunois Charles de Plouarven at twenty years.*

While the brother and sister were exchanging their thoughts before these portraits, the count entered the drawing room.

'We are rambling on about you, Dunois,' said his mother, smiling at him.

'I have nothing to fear from such gentle critics,' said the count smiling, and hugged her.

Peasants had come with a big arch of flowers and leaves on which was written with roses: 'Hail to the day of your birth, may God protect you!' It was a token of the affection, love and respect of the village for the count. The count himself thanked them. What a day! We finished decorating the drawing room, the dining room, and two other rooms. I saw Jeannette just for a moment. She seems very happy, but she couldn't talk a lot to me, as she said, 'I am weighed down with work, mademoiselle,' and she hurried to the kitchen. That evening, the count and his uncle took me back to my house in the moonlight. The count thanked me a thousand times for having helped his mother with the preparations. The bushes seemed to have silver gauze thrown over them, so much did they gleam in the light of the night star. We were on horseback; not a star, but the moon illuminated the heavens with its gentle light. We went along the small river, the waters mirrored, the willows bent over to see their reflections in this clear mirror. The wind murmured softly in the leaves. It was beautiful; we hardly talked, and silence reigned. The count and his uncle said good bye and shook hands at the doorway.

18 November

Louis arrived this morning. My father and I had gone riding, and on returning we saw a horseman who had got down at our door.

'My God!' exclaimed my father. 'It is Louis.'

And we set off on a gallop. Louis came in front of us.

'My dear boy, welcome,' said my father, jumping down from his horse and hugging our friend.

Louis shook my hand.

'But I didn't know that you could ride a horse,' he said to me.

'I just learnt to a few weeks ago.'

'However she is an expert horsewoman,' added my father, tapping my cheek.

'Ah! That is obvious at first glance itself,' replied Louis, and came to caress Austerlitz.

'It is a superb half-blood.' We entered the house. My mother joined us in the parlour, she hugged Louis saying, 'I am very happy to see you, my child.'

Papa led Louis to the room prepared for him, and I went up to mine. At dinner, mamma handed over the countess' letter of invitation to Louis. He said that he would be delighted to accompany us. The count came to see us in the evening; he requested Louis to come and the latter agreed.

19 November

My father, Louis and I, we went for a walk across the fields. We left at eight o'clock and we returned only at eleven o' clock. Before lunch, as I was alone in the house, I heard a strong, male voice singing the famous song of Musset:

If you think that I will tell
Whom I dare to love
I could not, for an empire,
Tell you her name.

The song was interrupted, and soon Louis appeared in the small garden and I went down to it.

'Oh! Monsieur Lefèvre, why did you not tell me you could sing?'

'Oh, do you call that singing?' he asked pretending to be surprised.

'But definitely.'

'Really?'

We went in for dinner. Tomorrow is the feast.

20 November

What a day it will be today! Louis asked my father if he was supposed to go in his uniform to the castle.

'Definitely, my dear man. You belong to the army now. When you will be an old retired person like myself, you can do what you like.'

We leave early after breakfast so that we can be present at the games of the peasants and their families. There will be a grand lunch for them on the lawns. I have to stop here.

21 November

Yesterday went off well. When we reached, the peasants had started to come. The countess was very happy to see Louis. The Goserelles were there, and all the families around. We crossed the drawing rooms. At noon, we arranged the tables for the villagers. We all came and sat on the terrace. The guests were split up in groups here and there. The count took me around the peasants. An old Breton, strong and robust, touched his cap and said, 'May God bless you!'

'Yes, may God bless you,' I repeated, seeing the gracious smile which touched the count's haughty firm lips, the softness of his black eagle eyes. He did not have a cap on, and the wind caressed his wavy hair and lifted it from time to time from his temples, white as marble. You cannot but love him.

I talked little, but I was happy to listen to his musical and joyful voice. He talked to each and every peasant, was interested in their minutest concern. We returned to the countess.

'Ah! How imprudent you are, Dunois,' she said to him, 'to go without a cap in full sunlight! You will catch one of your headaches, my child.'

She made me sit at her feet, running her hand over my hair. The count sat down close to us. I leant my head on the countess' lap.

'Everyone seems to be enjoying themselves, don't they, Dunois?'

'Yes, mother.'

'What time is it?'

'Close to three o' clock, mother.'

'Ah! How time has flown!'

We were there close to half an hour I think, when the countess said to me, 'What is wrong, my child? You are all pensive.'

'Nothing,' I said coming out of my reverie.

'But it is almost a quarter of an hour that you haven't opened your mouth!' she said smiling.

Mademoiselle Goserelle came towards us. The countess got up, and we went to join my mother. We remained outside until five o' clock, and then we went to rest a little before dinner. The countess led me to the room that I had occupied during my last sojourn in the castle. We gathered in the big drawing room. We admired the painting on the ceiling, we went into ecstasies over the decorations. I remained apart, looking out of the windows. A gentle peace seemed to have run in my veins, and I wanted to be alone. Mademoiselle Goserelle brought me out of my reflections.

'Do you know this military man?' she asked me, pointing to Louis.

'Oh, yes,' I replied smiling. 'This is Captain Lefèvre.'

'Is he a relative of yours?'

'No, an old friend.'

Louis came to me, and I introduced him to Mademoiselle Goserelle. As he sat next to me, Mademoiselle Goserelle appropriated him and talked of a thousand things, I don't know too well what! After dinner, there were fireworks. There is no dancing in the castle, and that pleases me. The countess hasn't given a ball since the death of her husband. Mademoiselle Goserelle was a bit shocked.

'But we cannot enjoy ourselves without a waltz or a quadrille,' she said to me.

'That depends on taste,' I replied. 'Each to his own.'

'Don't you by any chance like to dance?'

'Not much.'

'Oh! You are but a child!'

And having said that she went off for a walk with the Marquis de Merraigne.

We enjoyed ourselves till eleven o' clock, and only then did we return home. What a day! The peasants never got tired of shouting, 'Long live the count! Long live the friend of the people!' It was lovely to see them, the peasants, leaving in dark groups in the night, twirling their caps and cheering. The count accompanied us till the castle door. He covered me with a fur coat, 'Take care, and don't catch a cold, it is very cold,' he said to me.

The countess hugged me as was her usual custom. We said good bye and shook hands; the coachman whipped his horses and we were off. Today the count came to see if we were well. He, Louis, my father and I, went for a wonderful ride on horseback. How we galloped! The church bell is ringing eleven o'clock. I must stop here now.

22 November

We went for a ride this morning. We met Mademoiselle Goserelle and her mother; they were going by carriage to visit I don't know which Marquis of the neighbourhood. Mademoiselle Goserelle begged me to visit her mother as soon as possible; she also invited Louis who wanted to be excused from it.

'I would have been very happy to do so, but since I have so little time . . .' he said.

'You would love to spend this 'little time' with your friends, wouldn't you, monsieur?' replied Mademoiselle Goserelle, laughing. 'I thought as much; you have been made a slave of.'

That seemed to irritate him. He frowned and cast a look at me. Mademoiselle Goserelle noticed that he wasn't happy and said, 'Come on, Captain, don't look so fierce. You will come; Marguerite, make him come.'

'But,' I said looking at Louis furtively, as I had never seen him angry, 'if he doesn't want to come?'

'Oh! You innocent!' exclaimed Mademoiselle Goserelle laughing, and then added in a more amiable tone, 'If he doesn't want to, then you will come alone, my friend.'

She smiled, waved goodbye to us and went away. Louis had gone ahead of us, my father and I trotted along to catch up with him.

'Is Louis angry?' I timidly asked my father.

'No, I don't think so.'

'But he frowned while talking to Mademoiselle Goserelle, and at present he looks very worried.'

My father smiled. 'Louis,' he called out.

The captain turned around. His face had again assumed his gay and sincere look.

'What is it?' he asked.

'Marguerite thinks that you are angry. Is it true?'

'True, I was a little bit; this Mademoiselle Goserelle is a bit too witty.'

In the afternoon, when we were all in the garden, little Hélène ran in, all in tears.

'What is it?' I asked her, taking her on my lap.

'Oh, mademoiselle, little Pierre is so ill! Come and cure him.'

I tried to console her; my mother gave her a big piece of cake, and the child and I went towards her father's small house. There was nobody in the ground floor room.

'They are all in the bed room,' said Hélène in a soft voice.

I climbed the stairs, and I knocked on the door. No reply. I knocked again. Everything was quiet, so I opened the door and entered. Next to the chimney was the mother seated with the young patient on her lap. Monsieur Valpoine was close to the window; he was looking at his wife and his child with a sad look. Claude had his head on his father's lap. Monsieur Valpoine, noticing me, walked up to me and said in a low voice, 'You are really kind, mademoiselle; the little one is really ill, and the mother is afflicted.'

I went close to the mother and I knelt down beside her. The little one, pale, gave no sign of life, his eyes were closed. I went to take him in my arms, but she didn't want me to.

'No, no let him remain in my arms, he won't remain here very long.'

She sobbed.

'My God! He will soon be under damp earth.'

'God can cure him,' I said softly, and then she let me take the child in my lap. I covered his tiny limbs with warm linen.

'Monsieur Valpoine, won't it be a good idea to call the doctor?' I asked the father.

He looked at his wife. The doctor had already been, and held no hope. However, I sent Monsieur Valpoine to look for doctor Chanteau. After a few minutes, the little one opened his eyes, but they shut convulsively at once, the hands and feet were becoming stiff. I knew no remedy for children's illness, but I had heard my mother say that a hot water bath did them a lot of good when they had convulsions. I therefore bathed him, praying to God to cure him. When I had rubbed him with hot, dry linen, he opened his eyes. I gave him a spoon of hot milk, and he drank it.

'Oh! My Pierre is saved!' exclaimed the mother.

I put the little one in his cradle where he soon slept off. I recommended the mother to go rest a little, but she refused. We waited for the doctor. I thanked the good Lord for having saved the little one. Soon we heard footsteps on the staircase; the door opened, and the doctor appeared, followed by Monsieur Valpoine. They were told all that had happened; Monsieur Valpoine's eyes became moist. The doctor forbade me from waking the child. He gave us a potion to give the child patient as soon as he got up. While leaving, the doctor shook my hand; he was my parents' doctor even before my birth.

'Marguerite, you have a good heart.'

With that, he left. At six o'clock, my father and Louis came to fetch me. The child was still sleeping. I went down the stairs. Hélène was on Louis' lap and was telling him how Pierre was 'all cured.'

'I knew very well that mademoiselle would cure him', she said. 'She is so good.'

On seeing me, she ran and hugged me. Papa was delighted to hear that the child was better. I hugged Hélène, she then ran to Louis.

'And you, won't you hug me?'

He laughed and hugged her. We returned home. I went back to see the child. He is fully recovered. God be praised!

23 November

This evening as my mother and I were sitting in the parlour, we were looking at my father and the captain walking along the garden smoking cigars. They seemed to be conversing about something very interesting. I so remarked to my mother and she smiled.

'We must interrupt them, Marguerite. Go and get them back, for the coffee is getting cold.'

I ran outside. As I neared them I heard my father say, 'You are both too young, my son, but you can talk to her about it, when one is . . .'

I went and put my hand on his shoulder, he turned around abruptly and said surprised, 'What! It is you, my little one.'

It was a lovely moonlit night.

'I have come to get you back inside, my father, you and Monsieur Lefèvre. Mamma is waiting with coffee for you.'

My father took my hand under his.

'Let us take a turn. We will return later, my child.'

The captain had thrown away his cigar.

'Hey, Louis,' said my father 'you could have continued to smoke. Marguerite never complains about cigar smell. She is used to it; she even likes it I think. She thinks it is the duty of every good soldier to smoke. Her father told her that when she was young and when the smell made her ill, and Papa is always right, isn't he, Margot?'

'Not always,' I said smiling, for I saw that he was teasing. 'Not for instance, when Papa remains out, and lets mother wait for him with coffee, he is not right.'

My father tapped me on the cheek.

'Aren't you thirsty, Sir?' I asked the captain, who was walking by my side and seemed to be dreaming.

'One is always thirsty after a cigar, Mademoiselle Marguerite,' he replied.

'Let us go in, father. Monsieur Lefèvre is thirsty and so am I.'

'Why do you call him Monsieur Lefèvre, Marguerite? He doesn't call you Mademoiselle D'Arvers.'

'No, you do call me by my name, don't you?'

He smiled in affirmation.

'Then I will call you by yours, Louis.'

And I held out my hand to him and he took it in his.

'Let us go in, we have talked enough, my mother will be angry,' I said, and we went in.

My mother made me serve the coffee. I gave the first coffee to my father.

'The guest must be served first,' he said smiling.

'I started with the eldest amongst us, after you it is my mother, and then it will be Louis and me.'

My mother looked up at me, surprised at the 'Louis', and then she turned her eyes towards my father and he nodded his head.

'But it is you who told me so, father.'

Then I recounted to my mother how it came about that I called the captain by his name.

'But he doesn't call you just Marguerite' said my mother 'he says Mademoiselle Marguerite.'

'So should I say Monsieur Louis?' I asked. Louis replied even before my mother could open her mouth.

'No, please,' he said smiling 'I prefer just Louis.'

'Well then you will call me just Marguerite without the mademoiselle.'

'Yes, Ma . . .'

'. . . arguerite.' I added.

He blushed deeply. He was going to say mademoiselle again, I think.

24 November

Louis left us today. I fear that it is because of me. This is how it happened. This morning, very early, as I was plucking flowers to make a small bouquet for the table, Louis came and joined me. I could not give him my hand as both my hands were full of flowers. He smiled on seeing my embarrassment.

'That will make a lovely bouquet, Marguerite,' he said as I finished my task.

'Give me your hand, you haven't said good morning,' he said smiling.

I put out my hand to him.

'Don't the flowers smell good?' I asked and I held out the bouquet to him; he breathed the fresh smell in for a long moment.

'Give me a flower, will you?' he asked.

'With all my heart, but which flower would you like?'

'The marguerite,' he replied.

I looked him in the face to see if he was teasing, but he was not, he was serious.

'Really? Or is it just a compliment?' I said smiling.

'Absolutely true,' he replied. 'I love my beautiful marguerite more than any other.'

I looked in my bouquet.

'Ah! There isn't any, but I will go and pluck some, for Papa loves them too.'

We went to the cherry field, and there I made a small bouquet with the first marguerites that I found.

'Here, for you, Louis,' I said, giving it to him.

'The poor little girls in Paris run after anybody with their faded bouquets, and never stop crying out: "Flower yourself, monsieur" until you end up buying one, and then they fix it to the buttonhole of the person who bought it.'

He said this while trying to fix the bouquet to his buttonhole.

'Would you like me to do it for you?' I asked.

'How good you are! And how gauche I am!' he said smiling.

As I was tying the bouquet, Louis bent over to see how I was doing it. When I had finished, I looked up at him smiling. His face was all thoughtful and suddenly, in a voice full of emotion and very low, 'Marguerite, I love you so much, more than my life, more than I can ever say. Will you be my wife, my cherished spouse?'

I first looked up at him scared, but when he finished, 'Oh, Louis!' I exclaimed. 'Don't talk like that, it is not possible.'

I hid my face in my hands as I felt like crying.

'Don't you like me, Marguerite?'

His voice was dull.

'Yes, I do, but differently from the way you think.'

'Look at me Marguerite!'

I lifted my face, he leant towards me, and his face was pale with anxiety.

'Do you love someone else, Marguerite?'

Then, as I didn't reply, he added with bitter irony, 'Oh! I was a fool to place myself on par with him.'

With that, he went away. I watched him going away, he was already far off. I ran to him, I placed my hand on his arm. He stopped.

'Oh! Louis! Forgive me, don't be angry with me!'

He did not reply at once. The dead leaves detached themselves from the trees and fell at our feet, and then he took pity on my pale face and my tears.

'Can I, my child?' he said softly.

'We part as friends, don't we, Louis?'

'Yes. Oh, Marguerite! If you could have loved me we would have been so happy!'

Then, silence.

'Adieu, Marguerite!' he said.

'Must this be an adieu, Louis?'

'Yes, it must. I won't come back again, and I will never see you.'

I held out my hand to him. He shook it with poignant tenderness.

'Dear, little hand,' he murmured keeping it in his.

And then suddenly, as if obeying an irresistible power, he put his burning lips on it. The next instant, I saw him entering the house. I followed him after a few minutes, and I went up to my room. I knelt down close to the small cross in the alcove, and I prayed to God to forgive me and to make Louis happy, to bless him, to make him forget me and I cried . . . I got up and I sat near the window. Our servant, the old Adolphe, was entering the stable. He came out, holding Louis' horse by the bridle. So Louis was leaving! Soon, I saw him leaving the house, my father shook his hand, and my mother followed them. He said goodbye to them and mounted his horse, his face was all sad and beaten. My mother embraced him; my father again shook his hand. He left. I saw his figure recede; he neither turned his head, nor waved his hat. I was near the window when my mother entered. She had learnt everything. She sat next to me on the sofa, and I put my head on her chest.

'You don't love him, then, Marguerite?'

'I do, but not like that.'

There was a short silence.

'And you love another.'

'Yes, mother.'

And I smiled despite myself, for I thought of a gracious smile on severe, haughty lips, of two black eagle eyes, of wavy hair on a noble, white-as-marble forehead.

'Poor Louis!' said my mother. 'We so wanted him to be our son-in-law. But never mind. God does everything for our good.'

And then she added, 'Don't cry any more, my child, go wash your eyes, they are all red.'

And having embraced me, she left. No reproaches, my dear mother! Oh! My bad lost heart! Why give yourself to another without being asked? My father didn't say a word that would hurt me, he was only a little pensive. In the evening, when we all were around the fire, he remained a long time, his hand on my shoulder, looking at the fire in the chimney.

This evening, after having retired to my room, I sat near the window, looking at the misty countryside. Someone came in: it was Thérèse.

She began to stoke the fire, and then she approached me.

'Tell me, little miss, why did the handsome captain leave this morning?'

'Because it was convenient for him probably.'

'No, little one, he went away for your lovely eyes.'

And as I didn't reply, she continued, 'Listen to me a little, my little mistress, don't interrupt me. I suspected something when I saw him follow you with his eyes everywhere, and you, you never realised anything. This morning I was mopping the stairs when I saw him coming, his face all shattered, his hat rammed onto his eyes. He entered his room, locked his door. I remained dumbfounded and I very certainly heard him cry. You see, my child, how much he loves you! A quarter of an hour later, he came out, his night-case in hand, he saw me and said with a real sad smile, I assure you. "Adieu dear Thérèse." "Is the captain leaving then?" I asked in surprise. "Yes, Thérèse. Adieu." And then he went down the stairs and disappeared into the master's library.'

She stopped. I had my elbows on the window and my head in my hands. Poor Louis! He loves me as much as that! May God forgive me! A small hand tugged softly at my sleeve.

'Little mistress, you aren't angry with me, are you?'

'No, Thérèse.'

After a minute, she said again with a caressing voice, 'Write to him, little one, beg him to return. Just a small sign from your little hand will call him back. Make him happy, my good little mistress. You will write to him, won't you?'

'No, Thérèse. It is impossible.'

She sighed.

'But he will be very unhappy without you. He loves you to death.'

'Oh! Don't say that, Thérèse, don't say that.'

Tears filled my eyes, and I said again in a calmer voice, 'God will not allow it, my dear Thérèse. Doesn't he look upon us from the heavens? Doesn't he take care of us? Isn't he there to do good for us?'

'You were always right in whatever you did, little one. Goodnight, may the angels be with you.'

And she left.

The breeze became cold. The stars were all pale; I closed the window. Had I been offered the cup of happiness, and had I pushed it away with my own hands? Surely, not. How could I be happy with someone whom I did not love as much as I should? I love him as a friend, a true and faithful friend, nothing more. I feel I have done what I had to do. I reopened the window. The icy air entered the room sharply and seemed to enter my very bones. A vague premonition of great unhappiness took hold of me, and I shut the window again. I fell on my knees next to the crucifix. 'Oh, God! Be with us always!' I remained kneeling for a long time, thinking about all that had happened. I prayed to God for all of us, for Louis and for him whom my heart loves. The church bell is chiming midnight, it is time that I went to sleep.

27 November

Yesterday, in the evening, I was sitting next to the window in the drawing room; I don't remember what I was dreaming about, when I saw the count passing by. I wondered if he was going to come in, when I heard his footsteps on the steps. At the same time, Papa opened the door and made him enter the drawing room. There were no candles, the room was lit only by the fire in the chimney (for it has begun to be very cold, and we are obliged to kindle a fire in the evenings). Papa rang, and old Adolphe came in with the torches. The count shook my hand.

'You are a little pale, Mademoiselle Marguerite, I hope you are not unwell?' he said.

'No,' I replied.

'Ah! Your cheeks belie me.'

For my cheeks had coloured with the question that he had asked me of my health. We then approached the fire and the count asked for news of Louis. Slowly I stopped talking, I heard him talk to my father about politics, the most recent discoveries in geology, and literature, well, in short about all that he knows, and he knows everything! Then he requested me to sing. He went to open the piano and played a few melodious tunes on it. He started to sing the *Traviata*.

Di Provenza limar il suol

His sonorous voice echoed in the small room, and the last words of the first stanza seemed to die far away:

Dio mi . . . gui-da . . . Dio mi gui-da!

Then he started to sing in a softer, more touching voice:

Ah! Il tuo . . . vecchio ge-ni-tor . . . tu non sai quanto soffri . . .
tu non sai quanto soffri . . .

I think that I was sad for the thought of Louis, and his sad desolate look came to my mind and tears welled up in my eyes despite myself. I took advantage of the dark window embrasure to wipe my eyes without being seen. The song over, the count came to me.

'But you sing marvellously, Dunois,' said my father to him. 'My God! Grisi himself, in my opinion, could not have given more emotion and *soul* than you.'

The count smiled.

'Ah! You are too kind, General, and it is not you, who hears Mademoiselle Marguerite sing everyday, who should say this.'

And he begged me to sit before the instrument. I excused myself as best as I could from singing and I played the *Last Waltz of Weber*. When I finished playing, he exclaimed:

'Here is the most sad and pathetic waltz one ever knows. It is like the dying swan song or the last good byes of loved ones.'

He sat next to me and started talking to me of his mother.

'She adores you,' he said, 'and that is not surprising. You are so good, mademoiselle, and she too is good. And the good ones love each other, don't they?'

'Yes. But I am not good at all. As for your mother, she is an angel.'

Talking to him, being close to him, feeling his black eyes on me, breathing the same air as him, that is happiness for me; all my sad thoughts flew away.

'And your brother, why does he not come?'

The count's brow darkened a little.

'He is not unwell?' I asked.

'Oh! no,' replied the count smiling. 'Gaston is always well, and it is fortunate, for I suffer from these accursed migraines!'

He requested me to come and stay at the castle on behalf of his mother. My mother promised him I would. She told me that it would do me good. The count and my mother fixed the day. It is on 10th December that I will leave.

28 November

I went to see the Valpoines today. Not finding anyone in the small room, I was coming out, when little Hélène ran in from the back of the garden. She gave me two big kisses and then rummaging in my pockets, she found what she was looking for, and then she started chatting like a magpie while eating her gingerbread.

'Did you enjoy yourself, that day at the castle, Hélène?' I asked her.

'Oh, yes. And the count hugged me and he gave me a big piece of cake, as big as this,' she said showing a huge cauliflower.

'That was good of him,' I replied smiling.

'But,' she continued in a lower voice, and looking around her in fear of being overheard, 'but I will give him only one kiss even if he gives me all the sweets in the world.'

'And why is that, little one?'

'Because he is wicked.'

'Oh! Hélène, don't say that, it is not true.'

'Ah! But of course, it is true, what I am telling you. Mamma said that to Papa the other day.'

'Listen, Hélène. The count has a good and noble heart, he loves everybody. Does he not give you coins and sugared almonds?'

'Yes, and I said so to Mamma, but she shook her head and took me to bed for I was so sleepy. Should I keep half these sweets for Claude?'

'Yes.'

I thought of what I had heard. I was angry, thinking of him so good, so noble, and yet not being safe from meanness; but I thought mostly of Madame Valpoine, what ingratitude to say bad things about him, he who had done so much for the school! I had had a better opinion of Madame Valpoine. I was aroused from my thoughts by little Hélène.

'May I take one more sweet?'

'Eat them all, they are for you.'

'But you said that I must keep some away for Claude.'

'Really? I was thinking of other things.' And I gave her a small packet for Claude. I soon left her after having hugged her. My father met me in the garden.

'What is the matter, Marguerite? You look worried.'

I told him what I had just heard.

'You did not see Madame Valpoine herself, did you?'

'No, I was too angry with her.'

He smiled.

'That is strange, but I will never believe that you are capable of being angry, little one.' And he hugged me.

'I received a letter from Louis, Marguerite.'

'Is he alright?'

'Yes, he is, but he is a little sad.'

'Poor Louis!'

And tears came to my eyes. My father looked at me, surprised, but he seemed reassured seeing my eyes fixed on him.

'Oh! He will get over it, or perhaps,' he added. 'Our sentiments might change.'

But on seeing my serious face, he continued, 'Come on, God does everything for our good.'

30 November

Tomorrow we are leaving for Paris! Papa and Mamma had been thinking about it for a long time, but they had not breathed a word of it to me! When Papa told me, this morning, tapping my shoulder, 'Well, little one, go and pack, we are leaving tomorrow for Paris!' I remained dumbfounded; it was as if a bomb had fallen on me, Papa began to laugh.

'Look at her all dumbstruck! What is the matter, little one?'

I smiled.

'Is it true, Papa?'

'But of course, when I am saying so to you!'

I came to my room and here I am packing my trunk. I don't know when we will be back. Soon, I hope. I have never seen Paris, Louis had said so much about it to me! And my grand aunt! She lives there; we will most probably see her.

From my room I look out at the countryside which is desolate. All the trees are already bereft of their leaves, the sun has just set, and twilight lasts for a very short time. There is the count with his brother on horseback! Ah! He has seen me, for he is greeting me, smiling! He does not know that we are leaving tomorrow, or he would have come to say good bye to us. How spiteful people are to say bad things about him! Him, who will not kill a fly! What has he done to make people speak so disparagingly of him? He is so good! But he is strict too, he doesn't think of what people will say about him. He follows manfully the path laid down by his good heart and his upright conscience. I can still see him, riding slowly in the distance. Gaston is spurring his horse and is disappearing, but he, he has stopped, and then takes to the path at a gallop. May God bless him and look after him!

1 December

Here we are in Paris! Staying at my grandaunt's. She has welcomed us with so much affection! She hugged my father and my mother, and then she took me in both her hands.

'Ah! Is this young girl Marguerite?' she exclaimed. 'How you have grown! And how beautiful you are! You will turn every young person's head in Paris!'

That made me blush. My aunt turned her eyes to my father, who laughed a little and who, shaking his head, told me to climb up first. He, my mother and my grand aunt followed me a moment later. Aunt Genevieve made us stay with her; she would not listen to any refusal. In the daytime we went round all the galleries of the Louvre museum, and in the evening, Papa and Mamma went to visit an old acquaintance. I remained with my aunt; she began to talk with me very amicably.

'You have never traveled my child?'

'No, dear aunt.'

She stirred, and told me to go closer to the chimney.

'Come on, tell me about your acquaintances in Brittany. Do you know the Plouarvens?'

'Yes.'

'The countess is a widow and has two children, a girl and a boy, doesn't she?'

'No, she has no daughters, she has two sons.'

'They must be strapping young fellows by now. The eldest was called Dunois, I think?'

'Yes, aunt. Then you know the countess?'

'Oh, yes! Does she come to see you? And her sons?'

'Yes. She is very good to me; she loves me a lot, she requests me on and off to go spend a few days with her. There was a big feast at the castle last month, the day of the count's birthday.'

'Her elder son?'

'Yes, my aunt.'

'And does Dunois come to your house?'

'Yes, often.'

'Everyday?'

'Oh, no!' I said smiling. 'He has so much to do!'

'And he finds you pretty and kind, doesn't he, my little one?' said my aunt with a mischievous grin.

I blushed to the roots of my hair. 'I don't know.'

She began to laugh.

'All the better! Your old aunt finds you beautiful, and that should suffice!'

She showed me her album of photographs; I recognised the picture of Louis.

'It is Captain Lefèvre, isn't it aunt?'

'Yes, it is him. So you recognise him, do you?'

'Oh, yes! He was our guest in Britanny.'

'He used to come often to see me, but it has been two months since I saw him.'

It struck ten o' clock and my aunt sent me to bed. I wanted to wait up for my father and mother but she didn't agree to that.

'You will lose those roses,' she said tapping my cheeks, 'if you sleep late.' She took me to the second floor; a dressing room came before the bedroom, both of which were elegantly furnished. My aunt hugged me and went out. The fire was blazing in the chimney. I undressed and enveloping myself in a dressing gown I knelt down at the foot of my bed. I went to bed and fell asleep at once.

3 December

Papa had invited a painter, Monsieur Reyner, to come yesterday to make my portrait. The artist took but one sketch from which he will make the oil painting. We will leave after the 7th. We went to see some of Papa's friends. I am so tired that I am dropping off to sleep.

4 December

Monsieur Reyner came again today, he is so assiduous! He is going to make a famous portrait, I am sure of it! It has been only four days since we left the country, and here I am already longing to go back. This evening I was standing before the window when I suddenly realized my aunt was close to me.

'Ah! Here you are all dreamy!' she said to me. 'One would think that you are thinking of some handsome pretender to your hand!'

I was grateful to the domestic help who had not yet brought the light, for I could feel my cheeks flushing. The sly words of my aunt embarrassed me.

8 December

We are back! We arrived at five o' clock in the evening. After dinner I retired to my room to rest a little. Day after tomorrow, I have to go to the castle. He probably doesn't know (I mean the count) that we are back, for he would have come to see us. Or is he perhaps unwell? No! Oh, no! Surely he will come tomorrow. I am so tired!

9 December

He hasn't come to see me. What has happened to him? I am feeling
very sad today. It rained the whole morning, and I could not go riding.
Papa and I started to read Molière. Papa laughed at the misadventures
of the bourgeois gentleman. As for me, I had no wish to laugh.

'But you are not laughing, Marguerite! What is the matter?'

'I don't know, father, but it doesn't amuse me today.'

Three o'clock in the afternoon. It was beautiful this afternoon
and Papa and I went riding. We met the count, he greeted us and came
and joined us. He seemed to be in pain. He didn't know a thing about
our trip to Paris! He said that he would come tomorrow to escort me
to the castle. We rode till four o'clock. The sun was shining through
the clouds. Papa talked of Paris to the count, who seemed to be listening
to him, but I clearly noticed that he was thinking of something else.
He left us near the hillside. He is ill, or something is making him sad,
for he didn't look back nor did he wave his riding crop as he usually
does before disappearing.

11 December

He came to take me. He came in a carriage with his mother. The sun
was warring with the clouds, it was very cold. The countess hugged
me affectionately. I entered the carriage and she made me sit next to
her. He seemed more cheerful now. His mother made him climb up
with us in the carriage. He came in and covered his mother and me
with fur. He closed the windows, and we went off at a brisk trot across
the deserted plain. When we arrived, the countess led me to the
drawing room. We sat there and talked of everything. Gaston had gone
out. I went up to my room and throwing my furs and my hat on the
bed, I went to the window. The whole area seemed deserted; the wind
howled outside, the tree branches bereft of their leaves were swaying
strangely. I turned away from the desolate view and sat in front of the
fire. I soon went down, and the count met me on the staircase.

'We cannot go out,' he said. 'Would you like to rummage in the
nooks and crannies of the castle?'

'With pleasure,' I replied.

He led me first to a big cabinet full of books and family portraits. The room has only four windows, which give it a bleak look.

'Here is the portrait of Dame Catherine, who died of love, and here is her brother, the saintly knight.'

He explained all the portraits to me.

'Would you like to see the underground passage?'

'Oh! Yes.'

'You won't be frightened?' he asked smiling.

'But of what?'

'It is so dark there and moreover it is said that a murder was committed there by Count Arthur de Plouarven, in the year of the Lord 902. Blood stains can still be seen there on the floor.'

'No, I will not be frightened with you,' I said.

His face had clouded over, but he smiled on hearing me. He opened the small door hidden by the panel, and taking my hand in his, he made me go underground. Daylight enters there only through a small grilled opening which lets in a faltering and strange light. The passage is long, very long, and it is almost night there, but with my hand in his I had no fear. After a quarter of an hour of walking, we saw a small door, very low, he opened it and we found ourselves in the fields. As it had stopped raining, the count shut the door with a spring.

'We can now breathe more easily this fresh air as we come out of here,' he said.

The wind was still blowing, and we returned quickly to the castle.

The village priest, Monsieur Recamier, dined with us. He is a good man, full of charity. He had been the tutor of the count and his brother, and he loves them like his own children.

That night, standing in front of the fireplace, I thought of the day's happenings. Soon I heard someone knock on the door, the countess entered, she sat next to me, and pulled me gently towards her. I rested my head on her shoulder, she is so kind and gentle, the countess!

'What were you thinking of, my child? It was definitely some sweet dreams, for your face was radiant with happiness.'

I did not reply, but I kissed the hand that was holding mine. She was *his* mother, it was she who had given birth to him, nursed him, brought him up; I felt an immense gratitude towards her.

'I am used to looking at my sons in their sleep before going to bed; I used to do it when they were small, and I haven't lost that habit. After having seen them I came to see you, for I love you like my own daughter, and you love me don't you? As much as Dunois and Gaston?'

'Yes, I love you a lot. Was the count unwell last week?'

'No, that is to say, not seriously. But why do you call him count? Call him just Dunois, my child, you used to call him by his name when you were four years old.' And she smiled when she saw me blush.

'Go on, go to sleep, my child, and may God's angels look after you.'

And after hugging me, she went out. I knelt down at the foot of the bed, and I prayed. I prayed to the Good Lord to keep us from all temptation and all things bad for us. I opened the curtains a little before going to bed. The whole earth was dark and gloomy, and the wind rustled against the windows. Only the sky was scattered with stars. What a magnificent spectacle! 'The heavens declare the works of God, and the universe shows the work of his hands.' How true are these words! One feels the full grandeur of these words on seeing the sky glowing with stars. I lay down on the bed; the whole castle was asleep.

12 December

Yesterday it snowed for the first time. I got up and looked out of the windows. The countryside was all white. My God! How beautiful it is! The earth seemed dressed in white like a saint, all that was black or dirty was hidden under this pure and shining layer. Soon Jeannette entered to light the fire.

'Good morning, mademoiselle. It is very cold and mademoiselle is an early riser.'

'Not earlier than you, dear Jeannette.'

She laughed and went away. At eight o' clock, I went down to the drawing room. I only found Gaston there. He was standing near the window and he didn't notice me at first.

'You are all alone, Monsieur Gaston,' I said to him.

Toru Dutt

He turned around.

'You cannot go out, if this weather continues, Mademoiselle Marguerite.'

Indeed the snow was falling in big flakes.

'No, but it is so lovely, that I am not vexed.'

'But you will get bored.'

'Oh! I don't fear that.'

Whereupon that the countess entered.

'Dunois is unwell, he has the migraine.'

That was sad.

'And he won't come at all?' I asked.

'Oh, he will. He is so imprudent. He doesn't take care of his health.'

The count himself appeared. He said good morning to me. He seemed pale, the veins in his temples showed up blue and light against his transparent skin.

'I could not sleep the whole night,' he said.

Gaston had left.

'Why did you come down, Dunois?' asked the countess. 'Lie down on the sofa.'

He threw himself on the sofa and shut his eyes.

'Your breakfast will be brought to you here, don't move, my child,' said his mother.

He smiled and agreed. Then we went down to the dining room. After breakfast, the countess was going to carry the coffee to her son, but I begged her to give me the tray. She at last yielded it to me and we entered the drawing room. He couldn't eat but he was very thirsty and he drank two cups of coffee with milk. Gaston came in for a moment, and then went out, despite the snow. It seems to me that the count and his brother are no longer good friends, for they hardly talked to each other the whole day. The count requested me to read aloud, if it did not tire me. I was very happy to be useful to him, and I started to read willingly. The countess went out of the drawing room for some work and I continued to read. Slowly he fell asleep, I shut the book, and I kept still so as to not waken him. Looking at the fire, I thought of what could be troubling him, for I could well see that he was displeased, and even in his sleep, I saw him shudder, and then he mourned softly. He was probably having sad dreams, and I was half tempted to wake him up, but at the end of a quarter hour, he slept more deeply and more peacefully. Soon his mother entered and on seeing him sleep, she came and sat next to me. She made me put my head on her lap, and all the while she passed her hands over my hair she kept looking at her son.

'He is handsome, isn't he?'

I did not reply at all.

'He resembles his father, but he doesn't have his patient character. I would like to see him married. If he marries a girl like you, I will die a happy person.'

I blushed. She saw it.

'So you love him, don't you?' she asked gently, and as I hid my face in her dress, she resumed

'Well, why blush? Isn't he worthy of you, and you of him? My heart's desire is to see you as his wife; he will then have someone to love him and to take care of him, like his poor mother.' She then raised my head and kissed me affectionately.

'Come, my child. I love you more than ever because you love my Dunois.'

Two tear drops rolled down her cheeks and fell on my hair.

'You will make a beautiful countess,' she said. We remained there, her hand holding mine, for almost an hour. Then the door opened briskly and Gaston entered. The countess placed her finger on her lips, but it was already too late, the count had woken up. He excused himself in confusion for having slept off during my reading. But I was happy that he had slept and I said so to him. He smiled and shaking my hand, he said:

'Any other would have been offended, but you have a good heart, Mademoiselle Marguerite.'

I ran up to my room and there I threw myself on my knees all happy! In the evening, after dinner, when I went down to the drawing room, I found the countess there and the count at her feet, his head on one of her knees. I was leaving when the countess called me back.

'Come; sit down on my other side, for you are like my daughter.'

13 December

This morning, when I went down to the dining room, I found no one there. Soon the countess arrived.

'Where are Dunois and Gaston?'

'I don't know.'

She then called the old servant, Arthur.

'Where are the young masters, Arthur?'

'I saw Monsieur Dunois and Monsieur Gaston go out, one after the other, early in the morning.'

'Really? That's strange! Let us eat, my dear, they will soon come I hope.'

Indeed as she was talking, her elder son entered. He seemed annoyed and angry; below his frowning eyebrows his eyes threw out bolts of lightning.

'How careless you are, Dunois! Where did you go on such a cold morning?'

'I thought an outing would do me good, mother,' he said trying to smile and to look natural.

'And where is Gaston?'

'I don't know,' he said curtly.

His mother looked at him, surprised and anxious. At that moment Gaston entered all radiant. Something disagreeable passed between them, for they did not even talk to each other during the meal.

The Abbot Recamier came to see us during dinner; he begged Gaston to accompany him to his house for he wanted to tell him something. Gaston wanted to be excused from it, but the priest insisted, and he yielded.

14 December

The count is unwell, very unwell. He said so to his mother, and I heard him. I was about to enter the drawing room when I heard his pained and pleading voice say, 'I cannot mother, I cannot, don't force me.'

And the gentle voice of the countess saying, 'You are unwell, Dunois!'

'Yes, yes I am, mother, so unwell, so unwell!'

So I came up here; I bolted the door. So he is ill, seriously ill. I feel as if some calamity was going to befall me. Oh! My God! He will not die! No, oh! My God! Save him! But he is still ill. Oh! His pained voice! 'So unwell! So unwell!' Lord, cure him, I beg of you, may he not die! I prayed for a long time on my knees, and then I got up calm and comforted. I went down to the drawing room. The countess was seated on the sofa, and he, he was leaning against her knees. The countess seemed preoccupied and sad. She tried to talk gaily on seeing me. Without a word, Dunois followed me with his big black eyes, which were full of a strange sweetness. I forced myself to speak.

'Do you still have a headache?' I asked him.

'No, thank you, I am tired, that is all,' he said sadly.

His mother got up and went away. I could clearly see that she was ready to cry. Soon Gaston joined us. He had gone out and had just returned. He said that the weather was very cold outside, and he came nearer to the fireplace.

'Why did you go out then?' asked his brother brusquely, looking him in the face.

'Because . . .,' he replied laughing and blushing a little.

I was very sad to see Dunois angry. I said to the countess that I would return home tomorrow; she did not agree to that and finally we have fixed the date of my departure for the 17th instant.

This evening, at ten o' clock, when I was about to go to bed, I opened the window a little, for the room was suffocating me, I heard Gaston's voice under the window gaily humming a roundel of Coran:

Shepherdess wearing a seersucker dress
Arch your back, so that the buffer gauze
Make your lace hips puff out
Here is the tassel, let us go, mademoiselle,
In your hair knotted like in Japan,
Powder the heart with a rose pompom,

Put on rouge near your eyes so mischievous
Then a patch, . . . and be natural,
Rosy shepherdess.

The singer moved away and the song died away in the distance, but from time to time, I still heard the strong and gay voice above the wind:

Then a patch . . . and be natural
Rosy shepherdess.

I closed the window, and I am now going to bed. May God save us from all evil tonight!

2 January 1861

How to write it? How to recount it? Alas! Alas! Please be God that I should have died before seeing what I did! Oh! That I may have been asleep underground before this! Surely Ecclesiastes is right, surely he had seen a lot of pain and sadness when he cried: I bless the dead more than the living! My God! What a sad story that I am going to write! Lord, we have sinned; we are lost like the sheep without pasture. Forgive us and take us back into your fold. He has killed his brother! He, who was so noble, so good, so lovable! Who led him to commit such a crime? His younger brother, the son of his mother! I would have wanted to die instead of this! Lord, forgive him! You will forgive him, won't you, oh my Lord? For You are merciful. He is ill, very ill. He did not commit this crime of his own will; the malady stronger than him pushed him to this sin. He loved his brother, he loved him affectionately, he never said a harsh word to him. Lord Jesus Christ! Forgive him! Purify him of all his sins and console him in his pain! I will write all.

It was the 15th of December. At five in the morning I was awakened by a gunshot. I got up with a start. I opened the window ajar, not a sound. I remained standing for almost half an hour; I was going to go back to bed when I thought I heard voices. I got dressed in haste and I went down the stairs. It was just beginning to become day. In the long and dark corridor, I could make out a group of people. On seeing me the old nurse ran to me.

'Oh! Mademoiselle! Save him from the policemen!' she cried out.

Then I saw the count upright between two policemen, his hands tied. The sergeant came in front of me.

'What are you doing?' I asked him, indignant. 'Don't you know that this is Count de Plouarven?'

He turned his head, on hearing my voice. The sergeant was going to reply when I cut him off.

'You are making a mistake, but you will answer for this.'

'Mademoiselle, I would like to be mistaken, it is but too true that the count has killed his brother.'

Killed his brother! I couldn't understand a word of it. I turned my gaze towards the count, his eyes wide open, fixed on the dining room door, his dilated nostrils, and his pursed lips, everything pointed to the feverish agitation he was undergoing. But I repeated in a cold voice to the sergeant that he had made a mistake.

'Would you please come in through here?' he said, opening the dining room door. I entered, and he followed me, and shut the door. My God, I will never forget what lay before my eyes. Gaston's body was laid out on the table. His lips were half open; his glassy eyes were inordinately wide open, his shirt, his clothes stained with black blood, and the right chest pierced with a bullet.

'And it is his brother who did this?' I asked under my breath.

'Yes, mademoiselle.'

'Are you sure?'

'Yes, mademoiselle. It was the count himself who gave himself up to us when we were making our rounds,' he said in a voice full of pity. I went out and approached Dunois. I placed my hand on his arm, and I looked at him. My God! What a change had come over him! His big, black dark eyes were flashing lightning; at his temples the throbbing of his swollen arteries could be seen.

'Dunois,' I said softly, 'you are unwell. Would you come with me?'

At the sound of my voice, he turned towards me, he looked more softly, and he smiled. My heart shattered. God in heaven, what pain!

'Will I come with you? But of course, willingly,' he replied.

But at that moment, his eyes settled on his tied up hands, he looked at them with a sort of distraction, and then like a child who is scared, he cried out, 'Oh! Marguerite! What is this?'

I untied his hands and led him to the next room. He let me. There I shut the door, and he threw himself on the couch, and took his head in his hands. I sat next to him and I looked at him for a while. Oh! My beloved one, I know now how much I loved you! I took his hands in mine; his hands were hot and feverish. I didn't say a word. We were like that for some time when we heard the gentle voice of the countess.

'What has happened? Where are my sons?'

Dunois looked up brusquely; his eyes settled on the door, he was listening.

'My mother!' he murmured.

Then I heard the other door being open, the dining room door. A harrowing cry made Dunois start, and then I heard a voice full of anguish: 'Oh! Gaston! My son, my child!'

Then there were sobs, whispers, and then all went silent. I got up, he had closed his eyes at the cry, and a slight movement made him tremble, but that was all. I went out. The countess spotted me, and ran into my arms.

'Oh! Marguerite! What is this?' she said, crying as if her heart was breaking.

'Shh,' I said, 'he is in the other room, he is very ill, he needs his mother.'

She entered the room; she hugged her living son in her arms. I told the sergeant to go away with his men and then I entered the room. She was crying, but he, he seemed not to understand a thing, and was looking at his mother intrigued and surprised. I led both of them by the hand to the second floor, to the mother's room. There I wanted to leave them, but the countess would not let go of my hand.

'Stay,' she said, and I sat down next to her. 'Oh! Dunois, what have you done?' she asked her son, looking at his face, her eyes full of endless despair.

He looked at her, dazed, then he said in a bored voice, 'Let me sleep, mother, remove this fire from my head.'

She pulled him towards herself, he rested his head on her chest and shut his eyes.

'How he is burning me!' she murmured, passing her hand over his forehead.

His mother wanted to question him, but I forbade her. I sent someone to fetch the doctor. Monsieur Chanteau arrived soon after. I followed him to the drawing room. He made me tell all, when I had finished, he said, 'All that I have learnt about this unfortunate incident leads me to believe that he committed the crime in a fit of madness. Do you know the cause of this misadventure?'

'No, they were always very fond and kind towards each other.'

'Ah! There was no quarrel?'

'No. The count had seemed a little changed in his conduct this last month, but nobody seemed to have noticed it.'

He looked at me with a sort of pity mixed with kindness.

'Has your father come to know of all this?'

'I think by now he must know everything.'

After a minute's silence:

'Do you think I could see the count?' he asked me. 'I want to make sure of his condition, if one could prove that he acted in a fit of mental fever, it will be helpful to him the day of the hearing.'

The last words made me see the whole humiliation that was going to engulf him for whom I had been destined.

Ah! How much I love him! May God be of help to him!

Oh, Lord! Look at his troubles and forgive him his sins!

We entered the room of the countess. The doctor put on an air of unconcern.

'Well, my dear Dunois, we are a little unwell, aren't we?'

The count looked at him and smiled.

'I think so indeed,' he said.

'Let us see the pulse,' said Monsieur Chanteau.

During all this, he was observing Dunois with lively interest.

'Do you feel pain anywhere?'

'Yes, here.'

And he pressed his hand on his forehead.

'Ah! I understand, I understand. You will soon get well, I am sure.'

He questioned him some more with a few words gently and in an orderly fashion, then he went out signaling me to follow him.

'He is ill, seriously ill. He is mad. It will be good if you could watch over him, and especially make him rest. Don't talk to him at all about this affair. Do you know where his uncle is at present?'

I gave him Colonel Desclée's address, which was in Spain.

'I am going to send him a telegramme right away. He must come. But, my poor Marguerite, you must look after yourself, or else you will become ill, my child.'

He left me and I returned to the mourning room. Dunois had been made to lie down, and he was dozing. I signaled his mother and she came out. I told her all; she cried softly. Then we returned to the room; he was sleeping. How pale and haggard was his face! Suddenly he opened his eyes wide.

'Oh! the fire, the fire!' he murmured. 'This fire will make me mad! It is burning me!'

I took a handkerchief dipped in water and placed it on his forehead, but he rejected it. He pressed my hands convulsively. My parents soon came, and I went down to the drawing room. They wanted to take me with them; I begged them to let me remain. At last they yielded to my pleas. My mother wanted to keep me company, but I dissuaded her from doing so.

17 January

He is still ill, he has fever, he has been delirious for the past two weeks, unconscious of everything and does not sleep at all at nights. My God! How he is suffering! God have pity on us! His mother finally agreed to rest a little and we watch over the patient's bed turn by turn. The colonel came on 19th December in the morning, when I went in front of him, he took both my hands and hugged me, all moved. I told him what has happened.

'My poor boy, my poor boy!' he murmured. 'What will they do to him?' And then in a ferocious tone he exclaimed, 'No, he will not be judged, he must go away!'

He was stricken to the core. I remained silent and sad. Little by little he calmed down, he looked at me for a minute, then taking both my hands, 'You still love him?' I lifted my eyes to him without replying. He read my reply there.

'Poor child!' he said, and two large tears rolled down slowly onto his grey moustache.

18 January

Yesterday, Dunois spent a more peaceful night; he could sleep. At three o' clock in the morning, I was kneeling near his bed, when he placed his hand on my shoulder, half-rising and pointing to the window with his finger, he said very softly that I could hardly hear him, 'Jesus is He who died, who moreover was resurrected, who is to the right of God, and who *intercedes even for us.*'

He said the last words slowly, a smile of happiness on his lips. I was going to speak, but he silenced me.

'Shh! Listen!'

He seemed to see something, for he remained with his eyes fixed, his ears tended attentively. The stars and the moon softly lit up the horizon. A quarter of an hour went by, and then the patient fell back on his bed.

'It is over,' he said, a little sadly.

He shut his eyes and soon went back to sleep. The Lord is merciful. Surely he will forgive his iniquity. Who amongst us has not sinned? We all have strayed like sheep. We have turned away so that each may follow his own path, and the Eternal has taken upon himself all our sins. And God, our Father in heaven, does He not say thus: 'It is me, it is me that erases all your sins for your love of me, and I will no longer remember your sins.' Lord, forgive him his trespasses, make your goodness towards him admirable, and may his soul rest in you!

In the morning, the doctor was agreeably surprised at the count's state of health. At present the delirium is less, but the brain is weakened and hallucinating.

20 January

This morning I read near his bed. He had shut his eyes, and I thought that he was sleeping, but when I lifted my eyes for a moment, I saw his eyes fixed on me. He signaled me to come closer.

'I had a bad dream,' he said to me. 'Where is Gaston? He won't come to see me?'

I did not reply at all.

'Is he still angry with me? I want us to be friends, tell him to come, go on.'

I went out. Monsieur Desclée was coming up the stairs, I told him all and I added, 'Tell him the truth.' The colonel entered the room with me.

'Ah!' said Dunois on seeing us. 'He doesn't want to come?'

'He *cannot* come, my child,' replied his uncle in an emotional voice.

'Why not?'

'He is dead.'

'My dream is true then?'

He bent towards his uncle.

'I saw him, at the edge of the lake, and his eyes, what eyes, great God! Were all open, and as I came closer to him, a voice came out of his dead lips 'Cain!' he cried. His voice was raucous. Is that true as well?'

His eager eyes devoured his uncle.

'Yes, my child.'

'Oh my God!'

What a cry! He fell back on his bed as if dead. His uncle threw some water on his face; he opened his eyes, but soon shut them. The colonel told me to remain with the patient while he went to fetch the doctor. I remained there; a few minutes later, he opened his eyes again, and looked at me for a long time with an absentminded air; suddenly there was a flash of fright in his eyes. Dunois took my hand, and in a hoarse and low voice that I could hardly hear him he asked, 'Is it true that . . . I did that? Who told me that?'

I did not reply.

'Talk, you, you who speaks only the truth.'

'It is true.'

There was a deep silence. We looked at each other, silent, like statues of marble; a quarter of an hour thus went by when the doctor entered.

'Ah! You have become a dreamer, a visionary,' he said gaily.

Dunois seemed to come out of a dream.

'No joking,' he said. 'I know everything.'

Then there was silence.

'My God! Why didn't I die before shedding innocent blood?'

He sobbed, his head in his hands. The doctor and the colonel retired to the next room. I had gone to him, and instinctively I had passed my hands through his hair. Oh my God! How much he suffered! He calmed down slowly, he backed away from me.

'Think who I am, a fratricide!' he said bitterly.

A great sadness weighed down on me.

'Are we not the children of the God of mercy?' I said.

'Ah! You loved me, at one time, you did, my mother said so. Do you still love me?'

'With all my soul, may heaven have pity on me!'

'*Amen*,' he added.

He took my hands in his. After a silence:

'May God forgive me!' he said 'I have faith in His mercy.'

The doctor came in again.

'You need a complete rest of the body and soul'.

Dunois interrupted him.

'I feel completely recovered, Monsieur Chanteau, may justice take its course and may everything be in order. What day has been fixed for my trial?'

'The 22nd of this month.'

'And today is . . .?'

'The 20th.'

'The day after tomorrow then?'

'Yes.'

'That's good.'

He managed to sleep for four hours, despite all the events of the day.

21 January

This evening, Father Rochelle came to see the patient. After having read the fourteenth chapter of St. John's, he knelt down, so did we, and he prayed to God to forgive us our sins, to have pity on the patient.

'You, Lord,' he said, 'who do not want a sinner to die, but that he should repent and that he should save his soul, have pity on your servant, who calls for You from the bottom of his heart, and pardon him!'

We all cried. When the priest got up, Dunois told him, bending his head, 'Bless me, Father.'

Monsieur Rochelle placed his fingers over his head and said, 'May the Eternal respond to the day of your distress, may the name of God place you in a high retreat.'

The count told everything to his mother and me. When he started his narrative, I wanted to leave, but his mother told me to remain. He said, looking at me with a sad air which tugged my heart:

'Let her go, mother, the story I am going to tell you is sad, very sad, she should not hear it.'

But his mother kept me back.

'No, Dunois, let her stay, she loves you so much, the poor child . . .'

'Ah! She will no longer love me when she would have heard all, and then what will she think of me?' he murmured sadly.

The he recounted the whole.

'Here in a few words is what happened. I madly loved Jeannette Corraine, and he,' Dunois lowered his voice, 'he loved her as well. I had warned him ten times to get out of my way, to leave the path free for me. But he never took heed. As for her, she preferred him to me. I don't have the gentle manners of the other, she feared me, and even when I proposed to her to become my wife, she would have none of me! So something took hold of me. I no longer lived, and one night, it was a moonlit night, I saw them both walking along the path . . . that is all I remember. As for the rest, I don't remember a thing. Coward that I am, why did I not die before!'

He had hid his face in his hands and sobbed to break one's heart; his mother was also crying. I got up and I took Dunois' hands in mine. I don't know why I was like a dog, who sees the despair of his master, and who wants to console him and licks his hands. I saw clearly what had happened in the room, but I did not realise it; I was as if in a dream. He, he looked at me, scared of my paleness, he passed his hands over my hair.

'Poor, poor child!' he murmured.

Then he added: 'My God! Is she too going to die as well?'

'Go to your room, Marguerite,' he said softly after a short silence.

I obeyed him like a child. I climbed the stairs which seemed endless to me. On entering my room I sat down in a chair. I don't know how long I remained there; I was at last awakened from my torpor by an icy shudder that seemed to run through my entire body, I saw that the window was opened and that it was snowing. I shut the window. On turning around, like a consoler, the crucifix struck my eyes. I knelt down at its foot, I don't know what I said, but our Lord, who reads into the hearts, comforted me, for I got up consoled, a soul at peace. When I went down, I found Monsieur Desclée with Dunois. The colonel welcomed me with a hug. Dunois seemed beaten, but, on seeing me, his face lit up and he smiled at me, happy to see me.

23 January

Today is the day of the trial. I did not go to it; I did not have the strength for it. He, Dunois, went by carriage to it, with the doctor, his uncle, and my father. Some officers of the police accompanied the accused. He was very calm. May God have pity on us!

Evening. They returned at four o'clock. He was with them. His guards, on the insistent plea of his uncle, had agreed to grant him the favour of seeing us on the way and wishing us goodbye. I was standing at the door, my heart had stopped beating. Dunois came towards me, and, trying to smile, he took my hands in his.

'Sentenced to fifteen years of hard labour,' he said gently.

I did not reply. Sentenced to fifteen years of hard labour! Far from his own family! It was death. His health was sapped since this affair.

'Oh Dunois! That is tough!'

'No. Don't I deserve death? An eye for an eye.'

He became animated. I took him by his arm.

'Let us pray,' I said in a low voice to him. We found his mother in the castle chapel, prostrated before the altar, overlooked by an image of Jesus, His arms extended, above which was written this verse: 'Come to me, you who are tired of work and who are troubled, and I will console you.'

Ah! It was very heavy the burden laden upon us! We knelt down close to *his* mother; instinctively she had taken his hand and held it in hers. We did not say a word, but we prayed from the bottom of our hearts. At last he got up, and said in a very low voice, 'I must go now, mother.'

She got up sharply and encircled him with her arms.

'No, I will not allow them to kill my only child,' she cried distraught.

She looked around her, scared. He placed his hand gently on his mother's shoulder.

'I am only sentenced to fifteen years of hard labour, that is all. Pray to God for me.'

He detached himself gently from his mother's embrace; she fell to her knees before the altar. He bent over her.

'Embrace me then, mother.'

She threw her arms around her son's neck crying, and covered him with kisses.

'To the grace of God,' she said.

She again prostrated herself, and he turned towards me.

'Goodbye Marguerite,' he said.

Then, looking at me with his big black eyes, 'You will remember me in your prayers, like a lost brother, won't you?'

'Yes,' I replied. He resumed pointing to his mother.

'You will come to see her, when she will be all alone?'

'Yes.'

He took my hands in his.

'Oh, Marguerite!' he said. 'You have been so good to me, may God repay you!'

On that he went out. I would have liked to follow him, but all strength had left me, and I felt a hollow in my soul. Everything had turned black and dark around me; the light of my life was snuffed out. I was scared, like a child left without light and in the dark. I pressed myself against his mother. Oh Lord, help me and have pity on me!

10 April 1861

It has been a long time since I wrote in my diary. I have just got up from a serious illness. I had fever and was in delirium. They had no longer any hope of saving me. But God is good. When I opened my eyes, and I saw the sun, the blue sky, and especially the happy faces of my father and mother, I blessed God. 'All Your goodness is on me.' My life of the past is like a half forgotten dream. I will recount everything. I came to my senses only about a fortnight ago. Here is everything that I remember.

One evening, I noticed that many people were whispering in my room. I had my eyes closed; I opened them on hearing a noise. I then saw someone sobbing softly, on his knees close to my bed, his head in his hands. I closed my eyes again; I had recognized the curly and chestnut coloured hair of Captain Lefèvre. A sort of pain pierced my heart on seeing him. He had loved me from the first day, and what had I given him in return? Nothing but sorrow. A deep pity seized me, now that I was going to die, I had to beg his forgiveness for my wrongs. Here is what went through my head; oh! If only I had earlier recognised and accepted his love! I placed my hand on his lowered head.

'Louis,' I said, 'will you forgive me?'

I was very weak, and I could only speak with difficulty. As a reply, he took my hand in his and pressed his lips to them; his eyes were filled with tears.

'Louis,' I resumed, 'when I will no longer be there, you will be like a son to them, won't you?'

I then thought that I was dying.

'Poor mother, poor father! Take good care of them; they have the old habit of loving me, I only fear for them when they will no longer have me to devote themselves to.'

He did not reply, but he looked at me with such an air of inexpressible sadness and pressed my hands in his. I closed my eyes, exhausted. I felt someone embrace me.

'My poor child!'

'Father! . . .'

I must stop here.

After that, I had a relapse, but it has been three days since I recovered completely. I am still a little weak, that is all. I was left alone in my room according to my wish. Poor mother! She is so happy to see me on the road to complete recovery, even if I need some more time to get back my rosy cheeks of former days. This very morning she shed tears of joy and sadness on embracing me.

'How pale you are, Marguerite!'

Thérèse who was there, scolded her, all the while crying herself, even though she tried to pretend otherwise.

'Eh! Madame!' she said, 'that is a nice way to divert the little one. If you cry, she will start to cry as well, and this when the doctor has insisted that we should not get emotional'.

My mother smiled and passed her hand over my cheeks. Thérèse resumed, 'As for her pale cheeks, is she less beautiful for all that? On the contrary, I tell you, and I know someone who will agree with me when he sees her, and don't look at her like that, madame, and don't sigh either, because that will make her sad. Ah! When the captain will be here, we will be as gay as chaffinches!'

Papa entered at that moment. He came and sat down next to my bed and embraced me. Thérèse went out, mamma wanted to stay, but I insisted that she go rest. Papa added his entreaties to mine, and at the end, he put on an air of authority and ordered her to obey her husband. She at last yielded. He then embraced me, becoming all tender.

'My child is revived,' he said. 'Our God is merciful.'

'Yes, father.'

After a pause he resumed in a more natural voice, 'Do you know that Louis came to see you, little one?'

'Yes, father. I then thought that I was going to die.'

'Everyone thought so, my child, and the poor boy was so shattered on getting to know of your state from my aunt in Paris.'

Then he resumed after a long silence, 'He has gone to Paris now, but he will come to see you one of these days.'

'How is the countess, father?' I asked.

'Not well, little one, her mind wanders sometimes.'

'And him?'

'He is dead, Marguerite. He killed himself.'

'My God!'

I said that in a very low voice.

He put an end to himself in a fit of delirium. May God have pity on his soul! He has been buried outside the cemetery, far from here, near Toulon! And I, I want to join him.

20 April

Yesterday I was able to be carried to the drawing room. I wanted to walk down, but after a few steps, I had to sit down. Then Papa exclaimed: 'I am going to carry you, little one, you are too weak!'

He took me in his arms and laid me on the sofa in the drawing room. Mamma went to fetch me a glass of wine. Papa sat next to me; I passed my hand over his forehead, which looks more lined since my illness.

'Father, you really suffered during my illness!' I murmured.

'Yes,' he said, and strongly moved, he threw his arms around me, as if to defend me against death.

'God wishes me to stay with you, here, father, because I have not fulfilled all my duties towards you, and in his infinite goodness he has given me time to do so and to become a better person.'

He embraced me and did not reply.

21 April

Louis arrived yesterday. We, papa and I, were in the drawing room, when the door opened and even before old Adolphe could announce him, he was in the room. Papa gave him a cordial handshake.

'Where have you dropped from like a bomb?' he said laughing.

Louis came to me. I gave him my hand.

'Welcome,' I told him.

I saw that he was surprised to see me so pale and thin. Papa went to fetch my mother. Louis took my hand in his, and looked at my slender fingers, passing over and over again his hands over mine.

'How white and pale you are, Marguerite!' he said bending over me and lowering his voice. 'Poor little flower, you have gone through a tempest.'

He inclined his head towards me, his lips brushed against my forehead, he straightened up brusquely and went towards the fireplace. He was deeply moved, I could see that from the somber expression of his look. His eyes look all of a sudden completely black when he is moved. My father returned and mamma too. She embraced Louis, her eyes were filled with tears.

'Ah! She is very changed and very pale isn't she, Louis?' she said, running her hand over my hair.

'Yes,' he replied, 'but she will soon be stronger, when spring will come.'

'Do you think so?' she asked him sadly.

'But of course.'

And he smiled at me.

'Oh! We will undertake, Louis and I, between us, to make her recover within a week, what do you say, Louis?'

He strived to joke but his eyes were moist. Louis is going to stay here for a while. The evening passed off very well. Louis and Papa were each at one end of the fireplace, I was lying down on my couch close to my father, my hand in his, and mamma was working on her embroidery near us. As ten o'clock struck, papa said that it was time to go to bed. I got up.

'Ah! You will never be able to go up by yourself,' said my mother.

'You will see, mamma,' I said smiling. 'Did I not descend with just the help of papa's arm?'

Papa intervened.

'No, little one, it cannot be done. Climbing is more difficult than coming down.'

'Let me try a little, father,' I said.

I could only climb six steps; I sat down to get my breath back. My father came up to me.

'Oh! What folly!' he said. 'You will make yourself ill.'

'Oh, no,' I said trying to smile.

I felt really weak at that moment. Louis came towards us.

'Ah! Here is Louis, he will carry you to your room, little one.'

'Oh no.' I said.

'Bah!' retorted my father, 'he will not let you fall, you can be sure of that, young and strong as he is.'

Already Louis had taken me in his arms.

'Put your head against my shoulder,' he said very softly.

His voice seemed strange to me. I was tired, and I did as he wished. I felt so exhausted! When I opened my eyes, I saw only my mother, who was rubbing my hands, and Thérèse who was undressing me.

'She is coming around,' cried out the latter.

I wanted to get up, but Thérèse stopped me: 'What do you want to do now? A good fright you gave us all!'

I was obliged to remain still.

'I will inform monsieur,' said Thérèse, when she had enveloped me in a long and hot dressing gown. 'Where is he, madame?'

'There is someone walking in the garden,' I said, pointing to a figure striding about close to our chestnut tree.

'Ah! That is Captain Lefèvre!' replied Thérèse. And then she went out.

Papa came within a few minutes.

'You are very weak, you see, Marguerite.'

'Yes, father, but you see, I had come down in the morning, just holding your hand and I thought that I could climb back also alone.'

He looked out of the window.

'There is Louis walking and watching like a sentinel. He was very scared when he saw you faint, poor boy! How much he loves you, my child!'

Whereupon he bent over me and embraced me.

'Do you need anything?'

'Nothing, father. Go to sleep, and Mamma too, how much worry I give you!'

He embraced me once more and went out.

22 April

I was alone in the garden with my mother. We were looking at my father and Louis going away rapidly. Papa had mounted his own horse. Louis was mounted on mine. I wanted to dissuade him because Austerlitz, not having been mounted for a long time, was full of spirit. But Louis insisted, saying that he wanted to make him docile so that I could mount him when I had the strength. They left on a brisk trot and soon had disappeared from the horizon.

'Louis is going to stay a little while,' said my mother. 'He has a four month leave. I am very happy to have him at our home. He makes the house so cheerful! And during your convalescence you need to have cheer!'

'He is so good,' I said.

And I remembered how he had not made a single mention of the fact that I had refused his hand, last year, how with his very frank manners, his good humour, his friendly attention lavished on me for my well being, he seemed to want me to forget the past. My mother let out a small sigh.

'Your father loves him like a son; he would have loved to have him as his son-in-law.'

I turned my head away, for I could feel the tears coming to my eyes. My parents want me to marry Louis, and it is perhaps my duty to fulfill their desires. I had been quite wrong, and who knows if the good Lord had not cured me, to become a better girl so that I could overcome my own desires, so that I have some time to correct the wrong committed by me because of my stubbornness. They never talk to me about it, but I see it in their attitude. One must try to fulfill the smallest of wishes of such good parents. As for Louis, I still like him somewhat, and perhaps God will help me love him as I should if he marries me. God will guide me.

28 April.

Louis still loves me. I have promised to become his wife. It was yesterday. I was on the sofa, my back to the door. I heard someone enter, it was Louis. He came and sat beside me. He looked thoughtful, and when he lifted his eyes toward me, his sombre look pierced me to the heart. We did not talk at all. There was no noise outside, and this silence of nature extended to our hearts. His hand came out to touch mine. I foresaw what he was going to say. Then he spoke.

'Marguerite, I still love you. My life belongs to you. Be my wife, make me happy; oh my soul, don't refuse me, say yes!'

His voice was hoarse and his hand pressed mine with a convulsive hug. He was very pale, his look smouldered me. I rested my hand gently on his shoulder, I looked deep into his clear eyes, and therein I read his soul.

'Yes, Louis, I will be your wife.'

All the blood rushed to his face which had been so pale earlier. He bent over me and pressed his burning lips over mine, passionately, tenderly and for a long time.

'My God!' he murmured. 'How much I love you!'

And he drew me to his heart. A vague sense of happiness permeated me as I rested my heavy head on his loving heart. It was the same sense of happiness that had seized me when one day, when I was close to drowning (trying to rescue a peasant's small boy who had fallen into the river), my father had dived into the water and taking me in his arms, he had hugged me against his chest. It was no longer possible to see anything in the room; the shadows of the trees had lengthened over the lawn. We remained silent for some time. Then I lifted my eyes towards him, I met his luminous look, I took his face into my hands and kissing him on the forehead: 'Dear Louis,' I said. 'Do you really want me as your wife?'

My eyes were moist again. He embraced me tighter against his chest as his response.

'And what do you want of me? There is nothing but the remains of the Marguerite of before.'

And I smiled sadly looking at my thinned hands.

'From the remains we shall rebuild our Marguerite.'

My father entered, before he could say anything, Louis got up, retaining my hand in his.

'She has promised to be my wife, bless us, father!'

My father came to me.

'May God bless you, my child, you and the man of your choice!' he said, embracing me. 'You have made me so happy.'

'It has made you happy, father?' I asked smiling.

'Yes, yes, my child.'

He went to fetch my mother. She came and embraced me.

'Is this true, Marguerite?'

'Yes, mother.'

'So God has answered my prayers.'

They are happy, and I too am happy, more than I thought. God is good. Louis went out by the french window that leads to the garden, and we saw him walking and smoking a cigar in the small compound. My father took my hand.

'And you, are you happy, Marguerite?'

'Yes, father.'

And I embraced him.

'Ah! That is good. You see, it made me unhappy to see you so pale, now that you have hope in your life, now that you love, you will recover soon, this boy and you, you are made for each other. Aren't they, Henriette?'

'Yes, my dear, but the two young ones must be left alone so that they can talk.'

'Ah! Yes, Louis would like to send us to the devil right now, I think,' said my father smiling and getting up. 'There is so much to say to each other, isn't there, my child?'

And having embraced me, he went out followed by my mother. I remained lying down on the couch; I looked at Louis who was walking up and down. A few moments later, no longer hearing voices, he lifted his head, saw that the room was empty, and throwing away his cigar, he entered and came and sat next to me. He took my hand in his. I was dreamy. I thought of his strong and unchanging love for me.

'So when will it be?' he asked after a pause.

'What?'

'But the marriage of course!' he said smiling.

'Ah! Yes, on the day you fix it.'

'I would like it to be this very hour,' he said impetuously; 'let us fix the 13th of May, my pretty.'

'Yes.'

'That is a fortnight from now, it is a pretty long wait,' he resumed. 'I would like to see you being mine as soon as possible, my dear friend.'

'But I am yours ever since I promised to marry you, Louis,' I said smiling.

My reply pleased him, for he smiled and kissed me on the forehead.

'My gentle flower,' he said. 'I want to take you away to the Midi, far from the cold northern winds, to a warmer climate. You see, my flower will regain all her colour there.'

Tears came to my eyes at the gentleness of his voice. I am still weak, and even the smallest thing moves me. I parted the curls on his forehead, candid as a child's, and I looked at him.

'Well, what do you think of me?' he questioned laughingly.

'That you are too good and too handsome for me.'

And two big tear drops fell from my eyes onto his hands. My heart overflowed with happiness and gratitude, as he made my head rest on his chest and kissed me on my forehead. My heart had found its harbour.

5 May

Today I went to see *his* mother; she is turning mad, perhaps it is better that this is so, without this, she would have suffered too much. The colonel is staying with her. On seeing me, she came to me; I was alone. She embraced me.

'You are pale my child,' she said.

My God! Her soft gentle voice moved me strangely. I was ready to sit down and cry there.

'You were ill?'

'Yes.'

'Dunois will be very sad if he does not find you pink and healthy; he has gone out for a short while, he had some work to do at . . . where has he gone? . . . ah! I remember . . . Touloun! Ah! What a notorious city! Its very name fills me with horror, I don't know why, but that is how it is. I have become quite scared ever since Dunois left me. Gaston comes to me sometimes. I have such bad dreams at night that I am scared, and then I call him, and he comes.'

I was very sad to hear her talk like this. Colonel Desclée came into the room at that moment. He seemed moved to see me; he held out his hand and kissed me on the forehead.

'Oh well, my sister, how are things?' said the colonel sitting beside the countess.

She did not reply a word; she was lost in a dreamy silence. she was looking at me and seemed to forget herself in her contemplation of me. Suddenly she said, 'You no longer smile, little one; you are sad, what's the matter?'

'Nothing,' I replied, trying to smile, but my heart was heavy.

'You have lost your gentle gaiety. Oh! I know the reason,' she continued, smiling to herself. 'Don't be pained by it. Get your colour back, my child. Don't be sad; am I sad, me, who am his mother? He will soon return.'

I got up to leave. She embraced me again. On the landing I shook the colonel's hand, when he suddenly said: 'It is said that you are going to marry, Marguerite. Is it true?'

'Yes, it is.'

'And with Captain Lefèvre, aren't you?'

'Yes.'

He lifted my face to his. His abrupt tone made me sad, and I lowered my head to hide my moist eyes from him. His eyes met mine.

'Poor thing!' said the colonel with a distorted voice.

He accompanied me till the gate, silent and thoughtful. When the gate was opened, he seemed to come out of his reverie.

'Did you come alone, my child?'

'No,' I told him 'Louis is awaiting me near the castle boundary.'

He came out with me till there. Louis came in front of us. They exchanged a friendly handshake. Louis placed himself beside me.

'You are not tired, are you?' he asked.

'No, but let us sit down a little. The air is so refreshing.'

He was worried that I had overstretched myself. We sat in the shade of an oak tree. The colonel sat beside me.

'You are still weak, my girl,' he said.

Louis replied, 'Ah! She was so ill!'

'I know.'

'But she will soon recover her health.'

And Louis smiled at me. He is full of hope. He loves me so much! Only that I may be worthy of his love!

The colonel did not reply, but Louis did not notice his silence. He was looking at me smilingly, he was dreaming of our approaching wedding. After a little rest I got up, saying that it was time to leave. The colonel embraced me, he was very emotional.

'May God bless you, child, for all the kindness you have shown us.'

Then shaking Louis' hand, 'Make her happy, monsieur. Of course! You have chosen there a woman one does not meet every day. You love her, I can clearly see that, and that shows that you are a good lad. Perhaps we will never meet again, but you can be sure that the wishes of an old soldier will always be for your happiness, both of your!'

On that he left us. Louis and I returned home. It was already getting dark; my father was awaiting us.

'Ah! There you are!' he exclaimed and then hugging me, 'You are not tired?'

Adolphe brought along the lamp.

'You are pale,' said my father to me.

Louis, worried, came to me. I smiled to reassure them.

'Come,' I said, 'you never find my cheeks rosy enough!'

My father, reassured, embraced me, and Louis smiled. I went out of the drawing room to go up to my room. Louis followed me.

'Sweetheart,' he said softly.

He bent towards me, his lips met mine, and then I entered my room. After dressing up for dinner, I knelt down in front of the crucifix and I prayed to God. I had just got up when Louis knocked on my door.

'Come in,' I said.

'May I?'

'But of course,' I said opening the door. 'Do I have any secrets from you?'

He smiled and kissed my forehead. I made him sit down, and I sat beside him. My heart was full of peaceful joy; I had just asked God the grace to be a good wife to Louis. On lifting my eyes towards my fiancé, I saw his male face glowing.

'What are you thinking of?' he asked me.

'I think that you are a good man, Louis!'

And I put my hand in his.

'My Marguerite!' he said, and then he drew out of his pocket a small box, and took out from it a magnificent ring and slid it on to my finger. The ring was a bit big.

'Doesn't matter,' I said. 'It will not fall off.'

Louis showed me a lock of hair, black and silky.

'Do you know to whose tresses it belongs?' he asked.

'To your mother's?'

'No, to yours,' he replied smiling.

'But I don't remember.'

'That is very possible. I had cut it when you were so ill.'

'Louis,' I resumed after a pause, 'would you like to pray to the Virgin Mary with me?'

He got up and we knelt down beside the crucifix in the alcove, holding each other by the hand. We didn't say a word, but God can read into our hearts; He knows what is needed, and He gives it. We both got up moved, but happy. He embraced me for a long time.

'My wife,' he said.

'My husband,' I replied. We remained close to the window, silent, meditative; then we went down to the dining room.

11 May

My mother is very busy with the trousseau. I cannot help her; neither she nor Papa will allow it. Louis and I went to the river bank today. I sat at the foot of a tree; Louis threw himself next to me on the grass.

'When will we get married? That is what keeps going on in my head,' he said half smiling and half ashamed of his admission.

'But, day after tomorrow, Louis,' I said surprised.

'Yes, but . . .'

Then looking at me, 'Would you like to put back the date, sweetheart?'

'Oh! No! I will do everything to make you happy. I want to be good, you see!'

'But that you are always,' he said kissing my hand.

At that moment someone parted the bushes. It was Mademoiselle Goserelle, accompanied by a gentleman dressed to the nines. Louis got up with a start. Mademoiselle Goserelle started to laugh.

'I have come here at a very inconvenient time, haven't I, Captain?'

Then turning to me, 'I went in search of you at your home. I was told that you had gone out.' She added in a low voice and bursting out with laughter, 'I did not know with whom, or else I would not have interrupted you.'

Louis began to hit the grass with his whip, he was getting impatient. Mademoiselle Goserelle took my hand.

'But how you have changed! You look so pale.'

She introduced her companion to us as Monsieur Valines and told me in an aside, 'He is a rich heir; his father is a merchant and as rich as a Jew.'

And she continued louder, 'Were you ill?'

'Yes.'

'Ah! I didn't know that! I was in Paris. Have you ever been there?'

'Yes, once.'

'Do you hear that, Monsieur Valines? The child has been only once to Paris.'

Monsieur Valines smiled in an amiable, manner and bowing to me deigned to talk to me, 'If Mademoiselle comes to Paris, I am at her service to show her all that is to see.'

At that moment we heard several voices which were coming closer to us.

'Ah!' exclaimed Mademoiselle Goserelle, 'it is them. This way, Sylvie.'

Three ladies and two gentlemen made their appearance.

'Come, my dear,' said Mademoiselle Goserelle to one of the ladies. 'This is my Breton friend.'

Then addressing herself to me, 'These are my Parisian friends, Mesdemoiselles Briteve and Mariton, and Madame Carssa.'

She introduced the two gentlemen to us. All this talk made me ill, and I felt tired.

'We are going to have a party tomorrow on the banks of the river, would you like to come?'

'No,' I replied.

'Why no, so flatly? Come, say yes, you will come?'

Louis replied for me, 'It would be too tiring for her.'

'Then you will come,' she said turning to him.

'Nor me, mademoiselle, please excuse me.'

Mademoiselle laughed, 'Ah! Captain, you are always so farouche! But I will always be happy to see you. Do you want to come? No? How difficult it is to persuade you!'

She went away after shaking our hands. From afar she blew a kiss with her gloved hand.

12 May

This evening I was seated on the sofa close to the window, when Louis came and sat next to me. He circled me with his arms and I rested my head on his shoulders. I like being seated next to him. I know how much this male and sincere heart loves me; I know he will be my support against all dangers. I like feeling his cheeks brushing against my forehead, his hand pressing mine, my head on his shoulder. We did not talk. Tomorrow we will be united. Twice he kissed me softly on the forehead.

When Louis had just left me, my father came and sat down next to me and asked me where Louis was.

'There he is,' I replied, pointing out Louis who was walking and smoking a cigar. 'He went out just now.'

'Are you happy, my child?' asked my father in a very low voice.

I hugged him and replied: 'Yes, father.'

He was content.

'Louis wants to take you to Nice.'

'Yes.'

'It will be hard to be separated.'

'But you will also come, won't you, you and mamma?' I asked surprised.

'Later, my child. You must leave as early as possible this cold country; the air of the Midi will soon revive your health. We will come to join you in one or two months at the latest. We must settle our affairs here before leaving.'

14 May

We are married since yesterday. I gave him my word. When the priest put his hand in mine, I was all pale and troubled. May God give me grace to be a good wife! When we came out of the church, people threw flowers on our path. A verse suddenly came to my mind, I had read it somewhere:

All the paths would flower,
For the beautiful bride is going to come out;
Would flower, would sprout,
For the beautiful bride will pass by!

The last refrain is sad. Here it is:

All the paths would moan
For the beautiful dead lady is going to come out,
Would wail, would wail
For the beautiful dead lady will pass by!

Will this happen to me, to me? God knows. He will do what is good for us.

Papa and Mamma had gone ahead of us to the house. We were surrounded by people on all sides; some old folks blessed us loudly. They all love me, and have seen me grow up, and Louis, with his open male face had won over all the hearts. On the threshold of our door, papa and mamma were awaiting us. Papa embraced me affectionately, and then he embraced Louis as well.

Mamma encircled me within her arms; she was crying, but they were tears of joy. Louis was all emotional, but he remained calm. He embraced my mother, 'We entrust our only child to you, my son,' she told him. 'I know how much you love her and how happy you will make her. May God bless you!'

Thérèse was there and she flung her arms around my neck in her rush of joy:

'Go, my little mistress, go and be happy!'

Then, in a lower voice, she added: 'But, indeed, don't be so pale, my child!'

In the evening, the priest, the mayor and his family, the doctor with his family, and Madame Goserelle and her daughter came for dinner. They drank to the health and happiness of the newly married couple. Louis glowed with happiness. Mademoiselle Goserelle teased me, because I had not told her anything about the forthcoming marriage.

'Ah! Little imp!' she said. 'I saw you but day before yesterday and you didn't say a word to me about it!'

'I knew that an invitation card from my mother was awaiting you in your home.'

'And you thought that was enough!'

I retired to my room at ten o'clock. I was excused. I was so tired! My room had been rearranged for us, the door leading to the next room had been opened which would serve as a boudoir. Everything has changed in this tiny room where I have spent so many hours of anguish and happiness, only the crucifix is in it usual place. I knelt for a long time in front of it.

This morning I woke up late. At that moment Louis entered my room.

'Ah! There you are, at last awake!'

And as I looked at him with wide open eyes:

'You have already forgotten everything, my dear little wife?' he added smiling.

The words *my dear little wife* served as a ray of light to me and I looked at *my husband*. He was very handsome. He had placed his two hands on my shoulders, his male face radiated with happiness, his eyes were full of unending love, of boundless kindness, his rosy lips half open with a candid smile, showed his teeth as white as ivory, his brown wavy hair had gold and emerald lights in them under the first rays of the rising sun. I circled my arms around his neck and I pressed my lips on his. He sat down beside me and I placed my head on his chest. He parted the hair on my forehead, for they were half covering it, I pressed myself closer to him, and I lifted my eyes towards him, smiling, happy, confident. He was my husband, my friend; I blessed God for having given me one so good, so loving and so devoted. We prayed together at the foot of the crucifix. My husband went down first. When I went down I met him on the stairway as he was coming up.

'What's up?' I asked.

'Nothing, I forgot my watch,' he said, stopping short and embracing me.

He entered the room leaving the door ajar. Thérèse was coming down from the fourth floor.

'Ah! There you are, mistress,' she exclaimed. 'You are looking as gay and awake as a sparrow, even if you are a little pale, I say. Did I not always say that you will recover very soon!'

I smiled. Louis came out of the room.

'What is it, Thérèse?' he asked.

'I was telling mademoiselle that she will soon get back her rosy cheeks under your regime, Captain.'

'She is no longer a mademoiselle, Thérèse,' he replied smiling.

'How stupid I am!' replied Thérèse slapping her forehead. 'I must call her madame now. To think that the little one is already married! Ah! I have become really old!'

Louis laughed and we went down to the dining room. Papa welcomed me with a kiss and with a 'how is it going?' My mother smiled gently, she showed me a small box and a letter that were on the table.

'Are they for me?'

'Yes, Margot, from your grand aunt,' said my mother.

The box contained two magnificent gold bracelets studded with precious jewels.

'They are too beautiful for me,' I said smiling.

'Try them on,' said Louis. 'Let us read the letter first.'

The letter was full of good things for us. My aunt had sent the bracelets as a wedding gift, and she hoped that my husband and I would come to see her in Paris.

We went for a walk in the woods, my husband and I. I sat down on the green grass, shaded by the large branches of a cherry tree. Louis stretched out next to me, resting his handsome brown head on my lap.

'Louis, talk to me about your mother,' I told him a little timidly.

And as he remained without replying, I thought that my request had angered him.

'Are you angry, Louis?'

He lifted his eyes towards me, and his hand pressed mine.

'Angry! Why should I be? I was thinking how happy my mother would have been to see you as my wife, my beloved. She is seeing us right now, and perhaps she is blessing us from up above.'

'Do you have a portrait of her?'

'Not on me, I will show you when we return. I have on me a lock of her hair.'

He showed me a locket attached to his watch chain, which contained two locks of hair.

'The blonde one is my mother's, and the brown with the silver streaks is my father's.'

'She was blonde, your mother?'

'Yes, she was very beautiful, my mother, not at all like me,' he added smiling, and lifting his eyes towards me.

I bent down to embrace him.

'She was very young when she got married to my father, but not younger than you are, my darling little wife,' he added kissing my hand.

17 May

We are leaving tomorrow. That has made us very sad. My father and Louis tried to be gay, but I could see that my father was hardly that.

My mother was doing her embroidery beside me, I was stitching. She looked at me now and then, and then she wiped her eyes furtively. Poor mother! But she doesn't want me to stay here any longer for anything in the world.

'Your health needs a change of air and anyway, don't you have your husband with you? Why should I be grief stricken?' she said smiling.

My father came and sat next to me and took my hand in his. He said that my mother and he would join us soon in Nice. I checked my tears; I thought that would make them sadder. We will leave by the six o'clock express train in the evening.

I was in our room; I was crying. I could not leave the house, my parents, even if it was only for a month, without regrets. Thérèse entered.

'Ah! My child!' she exclaimed. 'Don't be so grieved! What will the captain say? He will be very sad to see you bathed in tears. Indeed no, one does not cry when one is going on a pleasure trip with one's husband!'

She made me wash my eyes in water. She is right, Louis will be sad to see me so grieved. Mamma came to embrace me in my room. She was crying. Then she gave me a whole lot of advice about my health, etc. She remained with me till ten o'clock. When Louis entered, she took him by the hand and made him sit next to her.

'My son,' she said to him. 'We have entrusted the happiness of this child to you, because we know that you will make her happy. Louis, take care of her, she is but a child, and so weak still!'

'Yes, mother.' She talked to him for a quarter of an hour and then she left . . .

19 May

We left Brittany yesterday evening. We arrived here at midnight. I cried a lot while saying goodbye to my mother and father; they accompanied us till the station. My mother clasped me tightly in her arms and covered me with kisses. My father embraced me; I clung to his neck crying silently.

'Go, my child, don't cry, it makes me sad,' he said in a low voice, his voice was trembling.

Then he added with a smile, 'Moreover, is there any need, in a young household, for old people like us?'

My mother embraced Louis.

'Keep her well, my son,' she said.

He shook hands with my father, who was leading me to our compartment. One more kiss, one more, 'May God bless you' and the train departed.

I kept looking at my father and mother as long as I could, then my eyes went to my village. I looked at it till it disappeared into the distance. I felt my heart go weak. I turned my eyes to my husband. I had just left everything for him, my parents, my country, my past. His clear eyes, full of tenderness, met mine and gave me a vague hope, of a glimpse of future happiness to come. I rested my head against his shoulder; I put my hand in his, and I sobbed noiselessly. He encircled me in his arms. By and by I calmed down, I lifted my head.

'I tire you, don't I?' I said.

'Me, tired!' he said smiling. 'Am I ever tired, Marguerite?'

The lamps had been lit, and then I noticed a man of certain years in our compartment. He seemed to be contemplating us with interest. I was very surprised; he had been a witness no doubt to my tears and emotions. I questioned my husband with a look, to know whether he had noticed the stranger's presence. He smiled affirmatively, and forced me to take the same position that I had just left. We began to talk in a low voice. In the silence that ensued, the stranger addressed Louis, 'Are you going to Paris, monsieur?'

'Yes, but just for one or two days, we are going to the Midi for a few months.'

The stranger glanced at me.

'I am going to Paris; I am a doctor, Doctor Laferme at your service; you are an army man, I can see.'

'Captain Lefèvre of the 22nd Light Cavalry,' replied Louis smilingly.

'Madame is not well?' asked the doctor courteously.

'She has just recovered from an illness,' replied Louis.

He looked at me with concern, the stranger's question troubled him. He asked me if I were tired.

'Oh, no! Not at all,' I said.

That reassured him.

We are staying at the Hotel du Louvre. It is six in the morning. I was used to getting up early at home and I have not lost the habit. When I think of my village, my father and mother, tears fill my eyes; however, I am happy, very happy. Louis is still asleep. I don't want him to see my tears. It seems to me that it is already a long time since I left my place, and to think it was just yesterday! We will go to see my grand aunt today. She is most probably not expecting us, but she will be so happy to see us. We will remain here only two or three days at the most. Louis wants to take me to the Midi as soon as possible. I prayed this morning before Sister Véronique's crucifix. I always wear it around my neck. She was very young when she died, she had just lived for twenty- six years in this world, and she had very little happiness and a lot of sadness, but now she is at peace. *Requiescat in pace!* Louis has just woken up.

'Am I late, my dear little wife?'

He bent towards me and embraced me.

I must stop here for he wants to talk over our plans for the day.

We went to see my grand aunt. When the servant announced us, she came before us.

'Come in, come in!' she said all happy.

We entered the drawing room. She took our hands and continued:

'Are you happy both of you? Ah! I don't need to ask! But, my child,' she said to me, 'you are so pale and have lost weight, were you so ill then? Poor little one! And the dear father and mother, are they doing well?'

She made Louis sit down, and led me to the sofa.

'Lie down there, my child, you must be tired.'

'Of course not, I am very strong. I am not a whit tired.'

She turned towards Louis.

'Is that true, Louis? You must dine with me then. Oh, no! No excuses! You must do what I want.'

I wanted to thank her for the lovely gift that she had sent me. She interrupted me.

'I don't want to hear anything about it,' she said. Come now, you both are going to have dinner with me, that will pay for my bracelets.'

We had to give in to her. She talked of everything, especially of our childhood.

'I knew very well that you would end up marrying each other. I will tell you how he fell in love with you, as soon as he saw you. It was his feast day, he had just turned seven, and you were two I think. There was a ball for the children; the room was full of children of every age, from two to twelve years old. Louis had in his hand a garland of flowers that he had to give to his queen of love. In vain did the little brunette girls and the gentle blondes pass in front of him; nobody seemed to take his fancy. At that moment, your mother entered holding you by the hand. Were you beautiful or what! With your white robe, your jet black curls and your big black eyes! He did not wait for you to come to him. He advanced towards you and placed the garland on your hair, accompanied it with a tender kiss! How we laughed! His mother, poor lady! She was in ecstasies. She took you in her arms, and asked you whether you would be her little daughter-in-law; you replied with a very serious and firm 'yes'. She was so good and gay, always laughing. She would have been very happy to see you two united!'

And my grand aunt wiped her eyes. Louis pressed my hand, and our eyes met.

23 October

Here we are well settled in Nice for the past six months. I like this coastal city. I have hardly written in my diary for a very long time, I did not have the time for it. My husband wants me to remain in the open air as long as possible, and in the evenings, I go to sleep before eight o'clock! I think that that is a very good indication that I am regaining my health! We walk for long hours on the banks of the Mediterranean. How wonderful it is, my God! The blue sea, under the sun's rays, is full of sparks that make me shut my eyes. In the evenings we often take our supper on the terrace. From there we can see the sea extending in the distance, and the waves reflecting the moon. We remain there for a very long time, he with his arms around me, and I with my head resting against his shoulders, my hand in his. Sometimes I fall asleep in this position, and then he lifts me in his arms and carries me to my room. I try to fight my sleep, I cannot, and I fall asleep despite myself. As for him, he swears that I am lighter than his epaulettes! He is so good, my Louis is, he loves me so much! And I am so happy to be next to him, to be his wife.

Neither my father nor my mother has come yet. They write to us every day. They say that they can come only next month. So sad! I had so much hope of seeing them before the end of August!

Louis is forced to go from time to time to Paris, where his regiment is. He absents himself two days at the most. He left yesterday morning for Paris. He wrote to me that he would be back this evening, and he forbade me to go to the station to wait for him, like the last time; he is scared that it might tire me out. But he has given me permission to go till the garden gate! I have something to tell him, something that makes my being tremble with gentle hope. Oh! How good is God!

It is six o'clock. Within half an hour, Louis should be here! I must shut my diary; I am going to wait for him in the garden.

24 October

I told my husband yesterday. We were on the terrace after dinner, he had just told me all about what he had done and seen in Paris. We had been silent for a while when I said in a low voice, without lifting my head from his chest, 'Louis, I think, that we are soon going to have a baby.'

He bent his head over me, his face brushed against mine; he pressed his lips against mine in an ardent kiss.

And since yesterday the face of the earth seems to have changed; nature seems to be revelling in my happiness. The birds which come and perch on the rose bush close to my window seem to sing more joyously, they look at me with their mischievous eyes and seem to share my happiness. The flowers themselves seem to bloom with more abundance, and when I am seated at the edge of the sea and when the waves come and murmur at my feet and wet them, you could say that they were paying homage to the man to come! Oh, God! Oh, God! How good you are! This morning, as I got up, I knelt down at Louis' bedside as he was still sleeping; I looked for a long time at his open male face; how much I love him! He is my husband, the father of my son! And to think that hardly ten months ago I didn't want to marry him! And he, he had loved me for a very long time! Oh! How ungrateful and wicked I was! But go on, I love you now, my beloved, 'more than my life,' to use an expression that you yourself used in the cherry field. I bent down to embrace him gently. Then I opened the window. The warm August light flooded the room. The sun with its radiant face seemed to wish me: 'Hello!' The birds repeated, 'Hello!' I would have like to shout my happiness at the top of my voice; I only murmured it to the roses that I plucked in handsfull. They were covered with pearls of dew, and I placed them at the foot of the statue of the Virgin Mary in our alcove; it was the offering that I gave her for our hope. I looked for a long time at baby Jesus in her arms; my son will be as handsome as little Jesus. I knelt down to pray to Him, I thanked Him for all the kindness He had for me. Then I prayed to Saint Virgin: 'Kind Mary, the mother of our Saviour, give me the force and the wisdom to bring up my child as an upright man, as a man after your son's heart, our Lord!'

25 October

Yesterday, we were in the drawing room which overlooks the terrace and from where we can see the sea stretch endlessly. I was on the couch, Louis was sitting close to me, his hand in mine, and we were talking of our child.

I said, 'He will be a soldier, Louis, like you, won't he?'

'If his mother so wants,' he replied smiling.

'Yes, I do want it so; he will be all like you, you see, he will be Louis Lefèvre the second. And he will be in the same regiment as yours, and he will serve under his father! And I will be proud of my husband and my son of the 22nd Light Cavalry! And when he will be twenty-one years old, he will be a captain like you, whereas you, you will be a Marshal.'

'Marshal of France?'

'But of course, without doubt. Aren't you brave enough for that? And then it will be you who will teach him to hold a sword and when he will accomplish his first glorious feat, everyone will ask: "Who is he?" and they will reply: "He is the son of Marshal Lefèvre." And I will say softly to myself: He is our child!'

26 October

Yesterday we went to the woods. After having got lost among the trees we entered our usual retreat shaded by olive trees and carpeted with moss. It seemed to be made just for us, this vault of greenery surrounded by wild rose trees. There I sat in the deepest corner and Louis stretched out next to me, his head on my lap, as we are used to doing. He looked at me in silence and played with the locket that contains his portrait and that I wear around my neck.

'I am going to sleep, sweetheart,' he said shutting his eyes.

I looked at him. He is very handsome, is my husband. His dark head stood out clearly against my white muslin dress. His left hand still played with the locket, his right one rested languidly on the moss.

Soon he opened his eyes and looked at me, 'What are you thinking of sweetheart?'

'Our son will be handsome, Louis, if he resembles his father.'

'If I am handsome, embrace me then,' he said laughing. I bent towards him. He passed his arm around my neck.

'Marguerite, Marguerite! How much I love you!' he said in a low voice.

At that moment we heard someone part the bush. Louis turned his head that side; soon a man appeared at the entrance of our 'retreat'.

Louis got up, 'Viart!' he exclaimed all joyous. 'What the devil brings you here?'

'The love of voyage,' replied the newcomer. 'But,' he continued, 'do you know what has kept me back in Nice? It is you and madame.' He greeted me.

'How come?' said Louis intrigued. 'I never even saw you since I have been here.'

'Ah! But you made such a pretty picture that I put you on canvas! You will forgive me won't you, Louis?'

'Forgive? Will I forgive you? It is flattering to one's ego to have oneself painted on canvas.'

'And madame as well,' he asked addressing me, 'Does she forgive me?'

'No doubt, monsieur, if there is anything to forgive, but I don't think there is.'

'Thank you, madame, you are too good.'

'But Viart,' resumed Louis, 'can one see this painting?'

'Not at present. Wait till I retouch it one last time. At this moment, it is but an outline.'

'Well, come and dine with us.'

'With pleasure, if madame is willing to receive me in the dress that I am in.'

'Go on! You and your Parisian polite manners!' said Louis.

And I added, 'All of Louis' friends are my friends, monsieur, and they are always welcome at our home, therefore no excuses.'

We took the path to our home.

'I didn't know that you were married, Lefèvre,' said Monsieur Viart.

'No, that is true; I haven't seen you or written to you for a very long time. We got married in May.'

'And you didn't send me even a word! Was that very friendly of him, madame?' asked Monsieur Viart, smiling and turning towards me. 'But I am not angry with you. On the contrary,' he continued, in a half teasing and half serious tone, 'I can well understand that one can forget everything when one has just got married, especially married to a beautiful and good woman like madame.'

Louis placed his hand on his friend's shoulder.

'You are not far from the truth, Viart,' he said with emotion. 'I am so happy now, so happy!'

His eyes veiled over a moment; his friend looked at him.

'I know that, Lefèvre, and I am very happy about it,' he said in a changed voice, shaking Louis' hand.

After dinner, Louis asked Monsieur Viart to sing.

'He sings like Mario, Marguerite,' said Louis to me. I joined my entreaties to those of Louis and Monsieur Viart sat at the piano. Louis sat on a chair near the window and I sat next to him on a cushion; he made me rest my head on his lap and placed his hand on my hair.

At the first notes of Monsieur Viart, a vague memory coursed through my mind; I knew the song, but I had forgotten it! Soon he started the song. Ah! I still remembered it!

All the paths would flower
For the beautiful bride will come out
Would flower, would sprout
For the beautiful bride will pass by.

It was a sad song, the song of Jasmine, which had come strangely to my mind the day of our marriage. Was this a warning, repeated twice? Listen! It is the end; the beautiful bride is carried to the tomb.

All the paths would sprout
For the beautiful dead lady will come out;
Would sprout, would sprout,
For the beautiful dead lady will pass by!

I felt my heart contract. I took my husband's hand and held it in mine. Like him, I am happy, my God, so happy. And the little one who is to come? Will I not be there to nurse him, to bring him up and to guide his first steps? Lord, if it is possible, may this never happen to me, not that my wish, but Yours may be done!

Monsieur Viart got up.

'Thank you,' said Louis. 'You haven't lost your voice. But you know other songs; sing us the beautiful Bretonne.'

'I have unfortunately forgotten it; I only know by heart this old song of Jasmine that I have just sung.'

He approached us. I murmured my thanks, and I went to the terrace on the pretext of breathing the fresh sea air. I didn't want my husband to see how much I had got affected.

After two or three rounds, I came back to him, more calm. Soon the lights were brought in, and the windows were closed. Monsieur Viart left us around eight o'clock, promising to come and see us everyday.

27 October

Yesterday, I wrote this in our room, it was eleven o'clock and I was scared that Louis would scold me for not having gone to bed. He was downstairs, doing his army accounts. I had prayed to God for a long time this evening. May He answer my prayers! A few minutes later Louis entered.

'Still at the table!' he said embracing me. 'Oh, my dear friend, you will make yourself ill!'

Then he began to run his hand through my hair.

'How beautiful you are, Marguerite!' he said.

I smiled at him.

'Have you finished?' he asked.

'Soon,' I replied.

Then I said, closing my diary, placing my hands on his shoulders and looking him in the face, 'You do love me, don't you, Louis?'

'Yes, you know that, dear child,' he said kissing me on my forehead.

'And I, I love you too, Louis, do you believe me?'

My eyes were filled with tears despite myself.

'Yes, my dear one, I think so.'

'Well then, will you forgive my past?'

'There is nothing to forgive, my beloved.'

I pressed my lips to his, and he embraced me for a long time. Then we knelt down at the foot of the cross and we prayed together as we are used to.

2 November

We received a letter from my parents; they will be here on the 9th. I am very happy about it. I spent the entire day arranging their rooms;

they will have two of them. Louis had started out by forbidding me to do all this by myself, but seeing that I could not remain still, he himself set to work with me. He is very happy about the forthcoming arrival of my father and mother.

Monsieur Viart came to see us; I told him that we were expecting my father and mother within a week.

'I will be delighted to make their acquaintance, madame, for your mother must be an excellent mother to have brought up such a charming girl.'

'Ah! You still have a pretty turn of phrase for a woman, Viart!' said Louis laughing.

'No, it is not just a pretty phrase; I say what I think, and what is a fact.'

I went after lunch for my daily visit to see Mother Jacqt. She is eighty years old and she is all alone. She likes me very much, and welcomes me always, when I enter her cabin, with a, 'May God be with you, my dear lady!' we talk a little; I sometimes take her a bottle of good wine, or a cup of soup, for she is very weak, the poor lady.

Today, as I was leaving to see her, I met Louis and Monsieur Viart. Louis came towards me and asked smiling:

'Little girl, in the white plains,

Where are you off to this early morn?'

'To Mother Jacot's.'

'I will come with you, Marguerite; come, Viart.'

We all went to the old lady's house. She was overcome to see 'two gentlemen' at her home; when I explained to her that they were my husband and his friend, she took Louis by the hand.

'Ah! Monsieur! You are my good lady's husband. I am very happy to see you, monsieur, saving your presence. She is very good to me, your lady, monsieur, and God will reward her for her goodness towards a forgotten widow.'

She became very fond of him.

'And monsieur is a military man? Even better. My poor Joseph was a soldier as well. He was my son, monsieur, but he remained there itself, in Crimea. That is all that I have left of him.' She pointed out with her head a soldier's dress, hanging on the wall.

'He was brave and good, do you know what was found on him? The medal that Marie Bolene had given him, and my letter.' The good mother wiped her eyes.

'She is now Madame Toussaint. I am talking of Marie, monsieur. She married the rich innkeeper of the road Massena. My poor Joseph liked her a lot. They were to marry at the end of the war. She is a good person at heart, Marie is. She takes care of me. It was she who made her husband buy this house for me. She comes often to see me. She has six children; she is a good woman and a good mother. Poor Joseph!'

She talked thus for a very long time. When we took leave of her, she shook Louis' hand.

'Doesn't the Good Lord hear the prayers of the widow? Well, monsieur, I will pray to Him for you and my good lady, all my remaining days here.'

9 November

They are here, my father and mother! They arrived yesterday. Louis and I were at the doorway; we were expecting them. At five o'clock, a carriage came to halt at the garden gate. We ran towards it. My father saw me first.

'Ah! There is Marguerite, she is looking fine!' he cried out.

My mother got down quickly and clasped me in her arms, then embraced Louis. She was crying, but with joy. My father kissed me several times; I clung to his neck.

'Dear father, it has been so long since I saw you.'

'Are you happy, Marguerite?' he said.

'Oh, yes, father! So happy!'

We said all this in a low voice; Louis came to interrupt us.

'What plot are you hatching?' he asked smiling.

'I was telling my father how happy I am, Louis.' I replied.

He didn't say anything, but I could read his thoughts in his eyes.

'Let us go in,' he said at last. 'It is cool, Marguerite, you must not stay out.'

I led my mother to her room. There she sat on the sofa and took my face in her hands. I remembered how the Countess of Plouarven used to do the same thing. Two teardrops came rolling down my lids. Was it regret? No, for I was smiling. My mother kissed me on the forehead.

'Do you love him now, Margot?' she asked me in a low voice.

'Yes, mother.'

'More than anyone else?'

'Yes, mother.'

She smiled tenderly. Her eyes were fixed on mine. She embraced me once again.

'Would you like to give thanks to God, along with me, for all His goodness?'

'Willingly, mother, you know that.'

We knelt down at the foot of the image of our Saviour.

When I entered the drawing room, I found only Louis out there, sitting next to the fire (it has begun to become cold), his feet on the firedog. He only noticed me when I was behind him, and had put my hand on his shoulder. He placed his hand over mine, and lifted his face to mine; the flames of the hearth lit his forehead and made his brown locks shine, his smiling eyes were full of happiness. I bent down to embrace him.

'You are alone; where is my father?'

'Upstairs, in his room.'

Then he got up.

'Sit down, my dear friend, close to the fire, you must be tired,' he said to me, making me sit on the chair that he had just left.

He positioned himself close to me, resting his head on my lap. We were like that for almost a quarter of an hour when there was a knock on the door. Monsieur Viart entered. He wanted to apologize when he found us alone and feared that he might have interrupted our tête à tête.

'Come in then,' said Louis to him, laughing, and without leaving his position, he put out his hand to him, and made him sit down near us.

Monsieur Viart said that he knew my father had arrived and that he had come this evening to meet him.

'But, you, Lefèvre, are you ill?'

'Me! Not at all! I am making myself comfortable. You see, my friend, when I put my head on her lap and her little hand runs over my hair, I feel so happy that I don't want to talk.'

My father entered at that moment, and Louis got up and placed a chair for him close to me. I introduced Monsieur Viart to him, and we began to talk till my mother arrived. We then went down to the dining room for dinner.

18 November

We will leave Nice on the first of December. We will stay a few days in Paris and then we will go to our house in Britanny. I want our child to be born in my countryside, and Louis wants that too. One evening, we were sitting, my mother and I, in the drawing room, near the fireside. Louis and my father had gone out. We were talking about Britanny for some time. I asked my mother how the countess was.

'As usual, a little mad. Poor dear lady!'

'And her brother, is he with her?'

'Yes, he left the army and has come to look after his sister.'

I became very dreamy.

Suddenly, my mother said softly:

'Marguerite, you are going to become a mother, aren't you, my child?'

'Yes, mother,' I replied in the same tone, smiling and blushing with happiness.

She took my hand and pulled me towards her. I rested my head on her bosom.

'And when will that be?'

'I don't know, mother.' My mother smiled.

'Do you have his nappies and all the little things which he will need when he comes?' she added, still smiling.

I led her to our room and showed her what Louis and I had bought for our son. Mamma rummaged through the drawer.

'A pair of small boots! What will he do with them, the poor little one!' she said. 'And a velvet kepi, and a soldier's uniform! Oh, Marguerite! Ah! Come on, that is better,' she continued taking out a small packet of nappies. 'But he will need more things. I will supply his layette.'

I smiled.

'Fine, mother. You know these things better than me.'

She embraced me once again. We were interrupted by the sound of voices of my father and Louis returning. We were about to go down when Louis met us on the stairs. My mother shook his hand and went down.

'What is it, my dear wife?' he asked me kissing my forehead.

'She knows that we are going to have a baby, Louis,' I replied. 'Isn't it strange?'

'You told her then?'

'Nay.'

And he embraced me again. He entered our room and I followed him there.

'Louis, my mother told me that it will be in February. Is she right?'

'Yes, my friend, in February, if it pleases God.'

'Louis,' I resumed after a short silence, during which time he was playing with my hand. 'Louis, I want to be in Brittany when I deliver.'

I think that my voice was a bit sad when I said that; the refrain of Jasmine came back to my memory. Louis lifted his head abruptly and hugged me.

'Of course, my child, who will look after you better than your mother at this time?'

My mother must have talked to my father about our child to be born, for when I went down, my father embraced me and placed his hand on my head saying, 'May God bless you, my girl, you, your husband and the child to be born.'

Louis soon came down to us, and it was a merry evening.

20 November

Today we all went to Monsieur Viart's studio. He wanted to show us the painting, barely complete wherein he has painted us in our vault.

It is magnificent. He shows me seated at the back of the vault, my face a little tilted towards Louis, whom he has shown lying on his back, with his head on my lap, with one hand he is playing with my locket hanging around my neck. He seems to be smiling, whereas I look serious, with a gentle look of expectancy on my face. Monsieur Viart has called it 'A dream of love.' Louis found the work beautiful, and so did I. Monsieur Viart is leaving very early tomorrow morning for Paris. He came to dine at our place and to say good bye to us.

30 November

I went along with Louis to say good bye to Mother Jacot; she has been very sad ever since she got to know that I was leaving for Brittany. When we entered her home we found a tall lady there; she greeted us and put forward two chairs for us. It was Madame Toussaint, née Marie Bolene.

'Ah! My good lady is leaving tomorrow,' said Mother Jacot sadly. 'May all happiness go with her, my good lady! Mother Jacot will pray every day for you.'

We said good bye to her and I slipped in two pieces of gold into her hand. Marie Bolene got up and saw us till the door.

10 December

Here we are in Paris again; we will leave it the day after tomorrow. Louis does not want to do a long trip. He is worried that it might tire me out. He is full of care. Yesterday my grand aunt came to see us. She comes every afternoon to take a ride in the carriage with us, and in the morning I go to her place; she loves me a lot. Yesterday my mother could not accompany us, so that Louis and I went alone to her place. My father was at a friend's place. At the Bois de Boulogne my aunt wanted us to get down from the carriage. We walked for about an hour, and then Louis told me to get on to the carriage again.

'You are not tired?' he asked anxiously, and covered me with furs.

'Oh!' said my aunt laughing. 'I am not tired, I who am so old and this young woman, how could she be tired?'

'She should avoid tiring herself,' replied Louis, and he got into the carriage after her. My aunt seemed to think for a few moments, her eyes fixed on me.

'Ah! I understand now,' she cried out at last. 'Is it true?'

I smiled blushing.

'Here your colour is coming back to you, little one. Ah! I should have guessed it earlier, how stupid I am!' And she embraced me heartily.

'And to think that you, little one, are going to be a mother, and I, I am not even married! And when is the little rascal coming?'

'In February, aunt.'

'Ah! As early as that!' she exclaimed. 'That is why you are so pale. That is what happens when you marry at sixteen, you have a child even before you are seventeen! But embrace me then, little one.'

I did as she wished.

'He will be a great heir, your son. Won't he be spoilt by caresses!'

She talked in this vein till we reached our door, when she embraced me once again.

30 December

I am so happy to find myself again in my own country! The day of our return it was snowing. The whole countryside was covered with a white shroud, and the moon had silvered the landscape, the snow was dazzling white. Louis covered me with furs, and my father told me to cover my face with the hood. We entered the carriage awaiting us and the two black Perche horses set off at a trot. Thérèse was at the door. She was awaiting us. She embraced me, 'Here you are back at home, little mistress!' she said all joyful.

Louis shook her hand, and we entered the dining room where a big fire of twining shoots invited us to warm ourselves. Thérèse relieved me of my furs and my boots which were drenched with snow. Mamma went up to her room after embracing me; she had tears in her eyes, she was so happy to see me returned to the old home! My father and Louis went up to change their dress. Thérèse fetched slippers and she placed my feet on the fire-dog. I thanked her and she interrupted me:

'Little mistress! I am happy to see you again, you see, I am getting old, and I was telling myself: will the little one never return? But a glimpse of you has made me younger by ten years, and I feel young and strong enough to be the nurse for the little master who is coming. Aren't I your good nurse? Wasn't I the same to your mother? Well, and I will also be for your son!'

She talked and I listened to her with pleasure. Our son! I only think of him, and I thank God. Louis and I, we talk of him everyday. Mamma is getting his layette ready. Today Louis has gone to Nîmes; he will be away for a week. He wants to have leave for two months at least to remain close by my side. I was so happy to spend Christmas close to my dear ones! We went to church at eight o'clock in the morning. The whole village was there. And what a shaking of hands, and what kind words were bestowed on me! I knelt down before the altar, my heart filled with gratitude towards God. Passing in front of the creche where little Jesus was lying, I went down on my knees. I thought of my son who will soon arrive. Gentle Virgin, help me, and give me the strength and the courage to fulfill all the duties of a good mother towards my child! Louis had knelt down beside me, and when we got up, he clasped my hand, and his thoughts were the same as mine.

Monsieur Valpoine and his dignified wife came to see me with their children. Claude gave me his hand with the gravity of a man, but Hélène was embarrassed; she blushed and hid behind her mother, she however ended up talking with me. Little Pierre came to me as soon as I stretched out my arms to him.

I went to see the countess yesterday. Louis accompanied me in the carriage. He told me not to tire myself, and I entered the room alone. The servant, who was the old chamber valet of Count Dunois, let out an exclamation of surprise. 'Mam'selle D'Arvers!' he said. He led me to the drawing room. The countess was lying down on a sofa. Colonel Desclée was sitting close to the fireside; he was reading a newspaper, and did not see me at first, but he turned his head at the sudden movement made by his sister on seeing me.

'She is coming from the country where Dunois is, she will give me news of him,' said the countess. Coming in front of me, she seized my hands and looked at me smilingly, and then she led me to close to the fire.

'How is he, my girl? He will soon come to see me, won't he? You are not replying, tell me something then, your silence is killing me, child. Is it not true that he killed his brother?' she asked in a whisper. The colonel brought her back to the sofa.

'Lie down, sister, you are unwell.'

She smiled, and did as he told her to. He came and sat down next to me. He said that the countess' condition was worsening day by day. He spoke to me in a low voice.

'But it won't be for a long time, you see how thin and old she is.'

'Yes, she is indeed.'

And tears came to my eyes looking at her.

'Are you happy?' asked the colonel of me.

'Yes,' I said lifting my eyes towards him.

'God is good; he will reward you for all your kindness towards the dead.'

When I took leave, the countess got up and embraced me. The colonel led me till the carriage. He shook Louis' hand.

'You have made her happy, monsieur, and I thank God, for He knows how much she deserves happiness.'

Mademoiselle Goserelle came to visit me today. She was accompanied by an oldish gentleman. She ran to the drawing room where I was alone on the sofa, and embraced me in a friendly way, and then she introduced her companion, Monsieur Lacoste, to me. She added, 'He is my future husband, Marguerite. I don't make a secret of it, you see, unlike you!'

And she laughed.

'He is a banker and very rich.'

And as I looked at Monsieur Lacoste, who was laughing, she continued, 'He takes me as I am, he knows that I have a great affection for him, but also that the rolls of money have a part to play in my consent, isn't that so, Richard?'

'You are so spiritual, Hortense!' he replied laughing.

Mademoiselle Goserelle continued more seriously:

'But you, Marguerite, haven't you got back your strength? You were lying down on the couch when I entered, and you look a little pale, my child.'

A slight blush coloured my cheeks.

'I am not unwell, thank you.'

'But where is Monsieur Lefèvre? I call him the shy soldier!'

'He is in Nîmes.'

'Where his regiment is, isn't it?'

'Yes.'

'That is the disadvantage of marrying a military man, my dear, they are often obliged to be absent from home, and in times of war . . .'

'There is no war at present, and there won't be any for a long time,' I replied sharply. 'And,' I added proudly, 'the soldier defends his country, he is a patriot before anyone else.'

'Do you hear how she defends her husband, Richard? But when will Monsieur Lefèvre return?'

'In a week's time. He has gone to ask for leave for two or three months.'

'Which he wants to spend next to his pretty wife, doesn't he? I hope he will get his leave.'

When Mademoiselle Goserelle got up to leave, she invited me to her wedding.

'It will be on 27th February in Paris. You will come, won't you?'

'If I can.'

'That means: if my husband permits me, doesn't it?' she said laughingly. 'But I will send an invitation to him as well, and you will convince him to come, come on! He will do anything for a kiss from your rosy lips.'

8 January

A new year! Louis returned today, with his permission of three months' leave in his pocket. It seems to me that I haven't seen him for a long time! I was awaiting him at the threshold of the drawing room; papa had forbidden me from going down as it was very cold. I spotted

Louis on his horse, from afar. He climbed the stairway very fast. He threw his arm around me and clasped me to his chest for a long time. My father climbed the stairs.

'If one isn't in love at twenty!' he said laughing.

Louis turned towards him reddening a little, and shook his hand; papa kissed him on the forehead.

'Go on, my son, I am very happy with you! Did you get your leave?'

'Yes, for three months,' replied Louis.

My father entered the drawing room after having hugged me. Louis went up to our room to get out of his travel dress and I followed him there.

'My colonel is a good boy, my darling wife,' he said to me after hugging me again.

I was seated at his feet, near the fireside, and he was running his hand over my hair.

'When I told him that I need leave, he asked me for the reason. On my reply that it was for family reasons, he gave me permission at once.'

I spoke to my husband about Mademoiselle Goserelle's invitation. He smiled.

'You cannot go, neither can I, for it is just then that we are expecting the little one.' He bent over me and kissed me on the forehead.

11 January

I had a sad dream the night before last. I got up very scared and I looked at my husband. The flames in the fireplace threw a flickering light on his face. My God, how peacefully he slept! Two big tear drops flowed gently down my cheeks. Will God want me to die, when my happiness has just begun! I bent over and kissed my husband softly on his forehead. 'Darling little wife,' he murmured in his sleep, throwing his hand around my neck. I pressed myself close to him, and remained awake for a long time—my dream troubled me.

I spoke about my dream to Louis yesterday evening. It was ten o'clock, and I was seated next to the window in my dressing gown. I had just got undressed; I had drawn apart the curtains, the moon had lit up the countryside. Louis came in a quarter of an hour later, he came to me, and bending over me he kissed me on the forehead. I got up and we remained standing close to the window, looking at the dead leaves that were slowly getting detached from the trees and that came and brushed against the window panes with the whisper of butterfly wings. Suddenly I said, 'Louis, when the trees will flower again, I will no longer be there; I will be lying under the cold grass.'

'God forbid!' it came out of him involuntarily, as he clasped me to his heart. Then fearing that I may not have heard him, and putting on a teasing tone, he resumed:

'What ideas do you have, dear child? You are delicate, and the time for confinement is drawing near, and you think too much about it, and moreover, you were all alone last week, and you filled your head with all this nonsense during my absence, didn't you?'

He looked at me smiling. He tried to reassure me. The moon lit up his face.

'Perhaps, Louis. But I had a sad dream in the night, and I was scared.'

'Why did you not wake me up, my friend? It is not good for you to be scared, in your delicate state.'

'Ah! You were sleeping so peacefully that I didn't want to put an end to it. I pressed myself close against you, and you encircled me with your arm, murmuring: "Darling little wife" and that gave me courage.'

He kissed me on the forehead, smiling. I had rested my head on his shoulder, and he had his arm around me.

'Tell me your dream, child,' he said gaily. 'It must be pretty terrifying to have scared you, for you are brave, Marguerite.'

'I dreamt that I was alone, lying in bed, when suddenly there was a knock at our bedroom window. I got up, but I was tired and I was scared; I didn't dare open the door when I heard my father's voice that spoke to me from his room, "Open your door, Marguerite, it is your husband." I got up and I opened the door. Nobody. I went down to the drawing room, thinking that I will find you there. You were indeed there, close to the window, your back to the door; I couldn't see your face. I lifted my eyes towards you, and then you turned your head and looked at me. My God! It was hardly your face, it was the face of Death, and on that I woke up.'

He had listened to me attentively. When I finished, he said smilingly:

'Do I have the face of Death? Look at me well, darling little wife, and then reply!'

'No, in truth,' I replied from the bottom of my heart. He was rather the face of life, and seeing his eyes so full of hope and infinite tenderness, his smile full of unfailing love, his face radiating happiness, all my fears crumbled away, my lips brushed his, and involuntarily I murmured,

When you look like the moon rises,
Suddenly my dream
Will shine forth.

He smiled. 'Are those words addressed to me, Marguerite?'

And bending down, he kissed me on the forehead. Then he said in a more serious tone, 'And do you think, dear friend, that the good Lord will take away our happiness that is beginning just now? No, Marguerite. God who is full of kindness, will not do that.'

I did not reply. Who knows? God does everything for our good, even when it seems just the opposite to us.

EPILOGUE

She gave birth on 14th February. Her mother was not there. The general had accompanied his wife to visit an old friend seriously ill, who wanted to see her and whose house was a good two leagues away. Her mother did not want to go, but Marguerite insisted that she should, saying that she was feeling well. At four in the afternoon she went into labour. She was in the drawing room with her husband, who was writing next to her, and she was knitting. After a few minutes, she lay down on the sofa; her husband turned around. 'What's wrong, my friend?'

'Nothing. I am tired, that is all.'

He came and sat down next to her. He was worried, but he did not want her to see it. She put her little caressing hand into his, and he kissed her on the forehead. Silence followed.

'Louis,' she said at last. 'I am going to go up to our bedroom, I don't feel completely alright.'

She got up, the room seemed to spin around her; she sat down again.

'I feel so weak, Louis,' she said.

He carried her in his arms and placed her gently on a chair in their room.

'Remain here for a moment, dear wife,' he said. 'I will send someone to fetch your mother, and I will write a word to the doctor.'

He left her, and sent Thérèse to her. The old servant undressed her, trembling with emotion.

'He is going to come at last, my child, isn't he, Thérèse?' she said.

'Yes, mistress.'

When Thérèse had given her dressing gown:

'Give me the most beautiful,' she said smiling, 'I am expecting people, my good Thérèse.'

Three quarters of an hour passed by. Her pain increased, it brought tears to her eyes, and the servant left her to fetch hot water. She was sitting close to the window, her hands on her face. Soon her husband returned; he removed her hands from her face and saw that she was crying.

'Poor child! You are so young!' he said kissing her on the forehead.

Then he resumed, 'You are suffering . . . a lot?'

'A little, my friend,' she said making an effort to smile in order to reassure him.

She saw that he was worried. He sighed, and she added, 'But I will forget everything when I will have my child; we must suffer a little to win such a prize!'

Leaning against him, she reached her bed. It struck six o'clock, then the half hour. He got up and started getting impatient with the doctor, whereas she, seeing him get up, threw her hands around his neck; she was delirious.

'Don't leave me alone, oh Louis! Don't go away! I am so scared!'

And he knelt down beside the bed, she with her hands still encircling her husband's neck, leant her head against his shoulder, her breathing was coming in gasps, her tears spoke of her suffering. It struck seven o'clock, she let out a deep sigh, and fainted: the baby was born. At that moment, a carriage stopped close to the house. It was her mother; she had met the messenger on the way as she was returning. She entered the room; the captain got up, placed his wife's head gently on the pillow and went towards her mother.

'The baby is born, she fainted,' he said briefly and he went out. Her mother entered with Thérèse into the room. Ten minutes later, the doctor arrived. The captain led him to the adjoining room. He told him everything.

'Her mother is with her,' he added at the end.

The door of the bedroom opened. Madame D'Arvers came in search of Monsieur Chanteau.

'You can come in now. He is a handsome baby.'

The doctor and Louis entered the room; she remained with her eyes closed, as if sleepy, and motionless. The doctor felt her pulse. A good half hour passed by, despite the doctor's efforts, before she opened her eyes. Her first glance met her husband's, who was bent over her, totally upset. She smiled to reassure him. He kissed her on the forehead, and she placed her hand in his.

'And the baby, my friend?' she asked in a low voice.

Madame D'Arvers placed the little one in the father's hands, who placed him in the bosom of the young mother. She looked at him for a long time, an ineffable smile came to her lips. She kissed the forehead of the little one as one kisses a relic.

'This is our child, my beloved, ours.'

Then she added, with a charming smile, 'Kiss him, Papa.'

He knelt down and embraced the mother and child.

'May God bless both my wife and my son, and keep them in His care.'

As he got up, Monsieur Chanteau placed a glass in his hand.

'Make her drink the whole glass,' he said.

She wanted to get up to drink.

'Remain calm, my child,' said Monsieur Chanteau. 'You are too weak.'

She drank a little from the glass that her husband brought close to her lips.

'I cannot drink, Louis.'

'You must, my dear.'

She obeyed him docilely.

'Eat, drink as much as you can and even more, my child,' said the doctor. 'Otherwise where will you find the strength to nurse this little man, hmm? And a bonny baby like this will not be satisfied with a little, I assure you.'

The doctor left her, and entered the adjoining room with her husband.

'Well?' said Louis, anxiously.

The doctor whistled softly between his teeth as a reply.

'Speak then, Monsieur Chanteau,' resumed Louis impatient and worried.

The doctor placed his hand on his arm.

'My friend, have patience! I have known Marguerite ever since her birth. I know that her health is basically good and strong. That is something in her favour. She is young, hardly seventeen years old, that is for, as well as against her. On the one hand, she is too young to be a mother, on the other, youth is always strong; the dear child can always battle against illness and weakness, and come out victorious in this battle. Is she as strong as before?'

'The fever that she had in April, before our wedding, had weakened her and made her thin, as you know, and then in May our marriage took place.'

'I understand, she had not recovered all her strength.'

Monsieur Chanteau remained a few minutes looking at the fireplace, and whistling softly.

'Was she ill after your wedding?' he asked at last.

'No, she fainted twice, that is all.'

The doctor didn't reply; his small gray piercing eyes were intent on the anxious and saddened face before him.

'Come on,' he said, 'she will come out of this affair; she is young, that is saying a lot.'

Then in a more gentle tone, 'Come on, my friend, there is nothing to be afraid of. Don't get worried; I have great faith in youth.'

They returned to the room. Marguerite turned her head towards the door, and seeing her husband enter, she smiled.

'Why did you go away? Sit down there.'

She made place for him close to her on the bed, at the foot of the little one. He sat down.

'He is beautiful, isn't he?' she said.

She took her husband's hand and made him touch the baby's.

'It is as soft as snow, isn't it? And then he is so fat! Mamma says that one could mistake him for a six month old baby, and then, his eyes are so clear and deep, he doesn't show them often, the young gentleman. And his hair?'

'It is black, like yours, darling wife.'

'Yes, but he is all you.'

'Is that a compliment, sweetheart?' he said in a teasing tone.

'Yes, it is true. Ask my mother instead. Doesn't my baby resemble Louis, mamma?

'Not too much chattering, my child,' said Monsieur Chanteau, coming close to her to wish her good evening. 'Get some sleep.'

The baby interrupted him with a pitiful cry; the young mother looked at him anxious, and then turning towards Monsieur Chanteau with an intrigued look. 'He must be hungry,' she said.

'Give him your breast.'

She blushed with joy and pride.

'But don't get up often to make him feed, or else you will be ill.'

The doctor went out. All the candles had been put out. A night lamp and the light of the fireplace threw flickering lights in the room. The baby suckled; the young mother looked at him, happy and proud, an inexpressible joy made the blood mount her cheeks, when for the first time she felt her baby press her breast, her husband seated beside her, his hand on the shoulder of his young wife, contemplating her happiness, smiling. At last the baby went to sleep, his rosy mouth wet and white with milk let go of the breast.

At that moment the general entered. He came to her.

'So, I am a grandfather from this evening on,' he said.

'No, don't disturb yourself, my son,' he said as Louis got up from his place close to the bed. 'Remain seated.'

He kissed his daughter on her forehead.

'May God bless you, my child,' he said moved.

Then sitting down: 'Well! How do you feel, Marguerite? Very weak, aren't you?'

'A little only, father,' she said. 'But you haven't as yet asked to see your grandson,' she added in a reproachful tone.

'A grandson!' said the general. 'To think that I am already a grandfather! I would never have allowed Monsieur Louis to marry you if I had known that I would have met with this affront before being sixty years old! At this rate, I will soon be a great grandfather!'

She laughed. Her silvery joyful laugh gladdened the heart. She ordered her husband to light three candles, so that 'Papa can see our child.'

The grandfather contemplated for a long time the sleeping face, visions of his youth came to him; he remembered his joy when for the first time he had taken his little daughter in his arms. The bed with white drapes wherein was his wife with the young one next to her—he could see it in front of his eyes. He became tender; he bent down and kissed the child.

'This day reminds me of the day that you were born, little one. But your mother was stronger than you, you are too wan and frail. She wasn't as young as you either.'

'How old was she, Papa?'

'Twenty-five.'

'She was older than Louis even.'

'How old is he? Let's see. 1840 to 1862? He is twenty-two years old.'

And as if he remembered, 'Today is your birthday.'

'Oh Louis, how stupid that I remembered it only now!'

'But you have given him a wonderful gift, little girl.'

She smiled with happiness.

'I could not have got a better one,' said her husband kissing the sleeping child.

She took her husband's hand in hers and pressed her lips to it. After a moment of silence: 'Louis, has a telegramme been sent to my grand aunt?'

'Don't worry on that score,' said her father. 'I have just done that. The captain is too worried to do anything. But you must rest, my girl, we will talk tomorrow. Good night, and sleep well.'

After having kissed her on the forehead, he went out.

The next morning, she was well awake before everyone else. Louis could not sleep the whole night, not that she was unwell, but that he was anxious. He had remained standing before the fireplace, his back to the bed, and buried in his dreams, he was contemplating the fire, when a soft and beloved voice called out to him.

'Louis!'

He turned around—she was looking at him with her big black confident eyes, a tender gleam sprang from within their depths. He came towards her and kissed her on her forehead.

'You didn't sleep, Louis?' she asked.

'I don't need to, sweetheart,' he replied smiling.

'But of course, you do! You will be ill if you don't take care of your health.'

'Rest assured of the opposite, little one. But you, how do you feel?'

'As strong as a dragon, and so happy, my friend.'

She caressed her husband's hand; the wedding band drew her attention, and she smiled.

'I wasn't too happy when I gave this to you.'

'And now . . .?'

'And now I am, my beloved.'

He embraced her and kissed the child also, who awakened by this caress, was searching for the breast. Louis went to draw the curtain and open a window. When he came back to her, the baby was still suckling.

'He has a good appetite, the young man,' she said smiling.

'The appetite of a little ogre; he would eat his mother if he had the chance and the teeth!' replied Louis laughing.

The infant looked at his father and seemed to smile.

'Oh, Louis!' said the young mother. 'See, he doesn't hear a word you say, while you are saying bad things about him, he is smiling at you.'

And then she added, 'And then he is also a boy.'

'And boys drink more than girls, hey, darling wife?' he asked smiling.

'I don't know, Louis, he is our first born. I am very happy that it is a boy.'

'And so am I, sweetheart. But the next time, in a year's time, I hope that we will have a little girl exactly like you.'

'In a year's time, my friend!'

Her voice had a sad note. She remained in thought for a few minutes, and said after that, as if talking to herself, 'And my dream!'

'Your dream, little fool! You believe in dreams, do you?'

And he tapped her on the cheek.

She shook her head sadly.

'I don't want to believe in them, but mine was so strange!'

'But all danger has gone, sweetheart; it was the delivery that we had to fear. You came out of it victoriously with the prize in your hand.'

And he placed his hand on his child's head.

'Do you think that all danger is passed, Louis?' she asked, a sparkle of joy in her eyes.

'I am sure of it, sweetheart' he replied.

She pressed his hand, she believed him faithfully. She had full confidence in him, her beloved, and in all his word.

'Louis, read me something from the Bible,' she said after a moment of silence.

He opened the Bible randomly, and began to read what came to his eyes first.

It was Psalm CXIV:

I love the Lord, because he has heard
my voice and my supplications.
Because he inclined his ear to me,
therefore I will call on him as long as I live.
The snares of death encompass me;
the pangs of Sheol laid hold on me;
I suffered distress and anguish.
Then I called on the name of the Lord:
'O Lord, I beseech thee, save my life!'

Gracious is the Lord, and righteous;
our God is merciful.
The Lord preserves the simple;
when I was brought low, he saved me.
Return, O my soul, to your rest;
for the Lord has dealt bountifully with you.

For thou hast delivered my soul from death,
my eyes from tears,
my feet from stumbling;
I walk before the Lord
in the land of the living.

When he finished, she said in a low voice, 'The pangs of death encompassed me . . .I called on the name of the Lord. O Lord, I beseech thee, save my life!'

Then she said softly, looking for a long time at her son, 'The Lord preserves the young ones: he will preserve ours, won't he, my friend?'

'Yes, he will.' And he embraced her.

She was very happy and content the whole day. On the 16th, towards the evening, she went to sleep. The doctor came to see her, and finding her asleep, he wanted to leave and come back later; but she woke up at that moment, and looked at him with a frightened look.

'Well, my girl, what is up with you??'

'Fear!' she said, with a voice filled of terror.

Her eyes shone with an unusual light.

'Fear!' exclaimed the doctor, smiling. 'Tut tut! And of what, my child?'

She placed her hand on her husband's arm.

'I slept a little, didn't I, Louis?'

'Yes, darling.'

'And I dreamt again,' she said, with a look of dread.

'Tut, tut. Dreams frighten you madam?' asked the doctor. 'What would your child think if he knew that his mother is a scared little thing? Come, come, drink this in one go,' he added giving her a cup of milk that her mother had brought her.

She drank it in one gulp.

'Admit that you feel better.'

Then he added, 'Drive away these black thoughts, my child; it is not good to scare yourself in your weak state, but this is very common. I have seen hundreds of young mothers with similar ideas and dreams.

Sleep well, and good night!'

He went out, followed by Louis, who questioned him with his eyes when they were outside.

The doctor shook his head:

'She is overexcited; she will be more feverish during the night. Give her the sedative.'

'You no longer give hope, doctor?' asked the captain in a low and rough voice.

'No, I didn't say that. She can get out of it, it is not impossible, but what I feared has come: fever.'

He went down, but he came up again nimbly; he found Louis leaning against the railing in the landing. He placed his hand in a friendly way on his shoulder; Louis started and turned around in surprise, then seeing Monsieur Chanteau, 'Ah! It is you' he said.

'Yes, I came to tell you not to allow her to nurse the baby; I will send a wet nurse, otherwise the baby will fall ill. And it is very important that she doesn't think there is any danger, it would be very bad for her.'

Then shaking Louis' hand, 'And you, monsieur, don't get sad like this, there is nothing much to fear. Out of hundred young deliveries, about five die at the most. It is true that fever is dangerous, but all illness is to some extent. Good evening.'

Louis went back to his wife's room. She was talking to her mother. A bright colour suffused her cheeks, earlier so pale, and her eyes were glittering; she was talking animatedly and brightly, but in a low voice, for the child was sleeping. Seeing her husband enter, she turned towards him.

'Marguerite!'

She placed her finger on her lips to make him keep quiet, and pointed to the infant sleeping. He smiled and went to sit with her.

'Don't talk too much sweetheart, you will tire yourself.'

At that moment Thérèse entered, the door creaked and the child woke up:

'Ah! Thérèse, you have woken him up, the poor little thing,' she said in a reproachful voice.

Then caressing the infant and embracing it, 'Ah!' she said in a silvery voice. 'There, he only wants to drink or to sleep, the lazy little fellow!'

She got ready to nurse him, but her husband placed his hand gently on hers which was burning.

'Don't feed him, dear child.'

She looked at him with astonishment, and a little fear.

'Why not?' she asked.

'You have a little fever, dear friend, and during a bout of fever, the infant should not have your breast; he will become ill with it. You can feed him when the bout of fever has passed.'

He said this in a calm tone, almost gaily, but his heart was wrenching seeing the little face lifted to his, listening to him with painful attention. When he had finished, 'Poor little thing!' she said in a sad voice.

And she kissed him on the forehead. Two large teardrops fell softly on the child's face; she wiped them away furtively, but her husband had seen them, and he placed his hand on his wife's hair. She lifted her head after an instant; she was no longer crying; she affected a calmness that she was far from feeling.

'And who will feed him?' she asked.

'Monsieur Chanteau promised to send a nurse immediately.'

Then he added, 'It will only be for three or four days at the most.'

The whole evening she was feverish, but she did not complain for even a moment. Her only care was to hide her suffering from her husband, scared that she would increase his anxiety.

When the nurse came, Marguerite looked at her attentively. She was a good peasant whom she knew well. It was Mother Ricard, the woman had three children of her own. Marguerite recognized her and placing her hand on the peasant's arm, 'Your milk is very fortifying, isn't it, good mother Ricard?'

She asked this in a soft, but so distressed a voice that tears sprang in the eyes of the kindhearted mother Ricard.

'Ah! Madame, you have seen my two older ones, aren't they strapping young fellows! And my last one as well, he looks two years old even though he is only one. You know that I have never engaged in nursing, but when the good doctor came in search of a nurse to our house, and when he said that the little mistress there was ill; and that it was for *her* poor child, I presented myself in front of him: "Here I am," I said, "a strong and healthy woman, doctor! I will be the young one's nurse." He was very happy, was the doctor. "You are truly good, mother Ricard", he said, but I interrupted him. "Can I forget that the little mademoiselle saved my little Guillaume when he was nearly drowned?"'

Marguerite held tight the peasant's hands as she wiped her eyes with the edge of her apron.

'Let us have a look at the little one, madame,' she said.

Marguerite placed the little one in her arms with a great many naïve recommendations. The nurse smiled at the naivete of the young mother who was telling her all the necessary care to be given to the baby. Marguerite looked at him feeding, while her hand remained in her husband's. Her dreamy eyes filled with tears, when she saw that the child had fallen asleep in the nurse's lap after having suckled for a long time. Her husband bent forward to kiss her on the forehead; she clasped his hand, and lifted her face to him. 'The infant will forget me when I will no longer be there,' she said in a desolate tone.

In the night, being unable to sleep, she asked to have the little one's cradle close to the bed. Her husband, thinking her to be asleep, had ended up throwing himself in the armchair to get a little rest, and he looked at her with a kind of suffering. The young mother's eyelids were shut, and her long, black eyelashes threw shadows on her cheeks. Her face was turned towards her infant; a sigh escaped from the chest of the young husband. She lifted her eyes towards him, 'What! You are not asleep, darling wife?' he asked her, surprised. 'What are you doing?'

'I am looking at our child.'

'It would be better to sleep, my friend, you can look at the child, when it is daylight,' he said.

'But if I die before that?' she murmured in a low voice, and as if talking to herself.

'Little mad one,' he said, kneeling down next to her and embracing her. 'Are you still thinking of death?'

'I so want to remain with you, my dear beloved, now that we have our child,' she replied.

'And who is to stop you? Not God! Death itself will not know how to take you from my arms.'

He talked brightly through clenched teeth, trembling lips, and kissed the young woman's forehead with passion. She smiled, but with little hope in her eyes.

'My beloved, my brave one!' she said with a sort of fervour, and she parted the curls from her husband's forehead, and looked into his eyes with love and confidence.

He got up and gave her the sedative, begging her to try and sleep. She slept at last, and on the morning of the 17th she felt better, even though the fever had not entirely left her, it had come down. The doctor came to see the patient. She received him with her gentle and charming smile, and the first thing that she asked him was whether she could nurse her baby that morning.

'You are impatient, my girl. Let us see your pulse and your strength, afterwards we will talk of the baby.'

'Ah! My little master has understood that it is about him,' he added, tapping the infant on the cheek.

He felt the pulse of the young mother, and became a little serious.

'You still have fever, my girl. You must not nurse the baby in your present state.'

Then seeing her disappointment:

'You will give him as much milk as you like once you are cured.'

'And that will be never, doctor,' she said smiling.

It was verily a sad smile. Later, pressing her lips against the child's forehead, she said, 'God will look after you, little one, and then you will have your father, but not the mother, not the mother!'

She turned her head and saw her husband, who, his face turned away, tried to stem his emotion, and her solicitude not to make him anxious at all prevailed in her.

'How stupid I am!' she said with her little silvery laugh. 'But, alas,' despite herself, in a forced manner, 'I have but a little fever, and here I am thinking that I am going to die.'

She placed her hand on her husband's shoulder.

'Go on! It is now you, my friend, who is having black butterflies; I have chased away mine. Don't get sad; I will hardly die; I don't want to, you see. Monsieur Chanteau, does one die of a little fever, and when one is young and strong like me?'

'Certainly not, my child. I am very happy to see you gay; try to be that always and tomorrow the fever would have left you.'

The doctor went away, promising to return during the day. At about four o'clock in the afternoon, she had a bout of fever. Her father came to see her; she was delirious. He embraced her tenderly.

'My dear father! Sit there,' she said to him, showing him the chair close to her bedside, and taking his hand. 'I will get well, won't I, my dear father? We will go to the Midi, to Nice, as soon as I am stronger.' And turning towards her husband: 'We will lease our little house,' she added. 'It is there for the first time that we spoke about our forthcoming child. We will go back and see Nice again, won't we, my friend? The child must see his countryside.'

Then, in a sort of fear, 'Where is the child? Give me my child,' she cried out.

She half got up from her bed.

'Shh, my dear wife. The child is here, next to you, don't excite yourself.'

He made her lie down again and placed the child next to her. She looked at him, he sought her breast.

'He is hungry,' she said with her mother's instinct. She hurried to unbutton her blouse. Louis stopped her, and took her hand in his.

'The doctor has forbidden you to nurse the baby at present, darling.'

'Why not?' she asked surprised, for in her fever, she could no longer remember the doctor's advice.

'Because you are ill, dear child.'

'Ill?' she asked, scared.

'Yes, darling.'

'Not too ill, am I, my beloved? It will pass. I will get well soon, won't I, dear Louis? Tomorrow?' she asked with painful anxiety.

'Yes.'

He could only speak in monosyllables. Monsieur Chanteau, who had been fetched, entered and came close to the patient.

'Monsieur Chanteau, I am not going to die, and I will get well, Louis told me so, and he only speaks the truth.'

And she pressed her husband's hand. Monsieur Chanteau felt her pulse.

'How do you find it? I don't have too much fever, do I?' she asked brightly.

'A little, my child, but you must try to sleep. I will give a soporific.'

'That will make me sleep?'

'Yes, my girl.'

'The whole night?'

'Probably.'

'And I will get up fully recovered in the morning, won't I, Monsieur Chanteau?'

'Not fully recovered, but certainly you will feel a lot better.'

He wrote out the prescription. Someone was sent to the pharmacist; she took the potion, soon she began to doze, and at last fell asleep. Monsieur Chanteau kept awake next to her husband close to her; her mother and father were also in the room. Her breathing was coming in gasps, her skin was burning, and even though she was fast asleep, she tossed and turned in her bed without finding rest. Nobody spoke. Monsieur Chanteau, with a newspaper in his hand, glanced occasionally at the patient, the mother rocked the baby, the father contemplated his dear daughter, his only child, with deep pain, then his sad looks were directed towards the young husband, who though calm, had the look of deep suffering etched on his face. He was kneeling at the head of his wife's bedside, and from time to time rested his head, tired and desolate, on the pillow. He kissed several times with infinite tenderness the little hand pressed in his: she had placed her hand in her husband's before falling asleep, then he softly parted from the forehead of the patient her black silky curls. Towards morning, at six o'clock, when dawn was beginning to lighten the horizon, she opened her eyes and half sat up.

'Louis, are you there?' she said, not knowing that it was he who was holding her. 'I can't see you.'

He bent over her.

'Ah! I can see you well, now, friend,' she said with her charming smile.

And she passed her little lean hand over her husband's face, and kissed him. Her eyes were wide open; her head fell back on the pillow.

'Give me our child, Louis.'

He held him close to her face; she contemplated him for a long time, then kissed him tenderly.

'He is sleeping,' she said. 'I would have loved to see his clear eyes before departing, but it doesn't matter. Keep him back in the cradle, take care not to wake him up.'

When the captain had replaced the infant in the cradle, she took the hand of the young father in hers.

'It is all dark. Come closer, friend, closer.'

She clasped her husband's hand tightly.

'I am so tired,' she murmured, 'so tired; I would like to sleep. Embrace me, my beloved, before I fall asleep.'

He embraced her.

'May God keep us in his care,' she sighed.

It was her habit since childhood to say this prayer before sleeping. She closed her eyes; her lips half opened, and her pure soul flew away to her God's bosom, and Marguerite slept the sleep of death.

ACKNOWLEDGEMENTS

This translation would not have been possible without the help of three French friends – Claude Guillot who introduced me to Claire Barthez who introduced me to Isabelle Riaboff. It is thanks to these three that I was able to procure a copy of the *Journal de Mademoiselle D'Arvers* from the Bibliothèque Nationale in Paris. They had to do extensive research before finding it under Clarisse Bader's name! It is entirely due to their efforts at finding, photocopying and mailing it to me, that I could read this work. *Un grand merci à vous trois!*

To Karthika, my profoundest thanks for having backed the project from its initial stages as also to Sumitra Srinivasan for her editorial suggestions.

I would also like to thank my literal and literary team mate G.J.V. Prasad without whose initial enthusiasm and constant prodding to undertake this task this work would never have taken off. My most sincere thanks go to my daughter Shubha who kept up a constant supply of tea and sulks that kept me going in front of the cathode tube.

And to my extended family of chilled out siblings and encouraging in laws I say a big thank you.

Last but not least thanks are due to my supportive parents whose unquestioning presence has ensured that the household was looked after when I was too immersed in my work to be bothered about it.